ONCE IN A BLUE MOON

A STORY FOR THE YOUNG AT HEART

R. S. Curtis

ARCHWAY PUBLISHING

This is a work of fiction. All of the characters, names, incidents, organizations, and dialogue in this novel are either the products of the author's imagination or are used fictitiously.

Archway Publishing books may be ordered through booksellers or by contacting:

Archway Publishing
1663 Liberty Drive
Bloomington, IN 47403
www.archwaypublishing.com
1 (888) 242-5904

Illustrations by the author

ISBN: 978-1-4808-8001-6 (sc)
ISBN: 978-1-4808-8002-3 (hc)
ISBN: 978-1-4808-8000-9 (e)

Library of Congress Control Number: 2019909841

Print information available on the last page.

Archway Publishing rev. date: 8/13/2019

For my wife, Martha Ann. You make me feel better, warm, and good. Never just okay.

Contents

Chapter 1

Anything Is Possible

It's that time of the year in the Rocky Mountains when the aspens have lost their leaves and the first snow of the season has yet to fall, that time when everything is about to be new and anything is possible.

—Dr. Gabriel Rainwater, Head Ranger, FUR,
Good Bear Lake, Colorado

Rainwater Island, November 1998

Snow clouds hide the full yellow moon above a small island in the middle of the dark blue waters of Good Bear Lake, the largest and deepest naturally occurring body of water in Colorado. The island is named for the Rainwater family, who have lived there for as long as the island has existed, according to the descendants of the early Native Americans who still live along the shores of the lake, in the foothills of Shadow Mountain. These are people with names like Sam and Clara Summertime, Bob and Lulu Big Sky, Dinky Round

Rock, Jack and Cleo Newday, Gabriel and Chris Rainwater, and Chipmunk Who Falls A Lot.

The Rainwater house and barn are located at the top of the island, above the flat stone steps that lead to the boat dock below. Both are ancient log structures, older than the tall trees that surround them, or as some of the native population might say, as old as the rock upon which they stand. The barn has large hand-blown windows that extend the length of its back side. Any light emanating from inside the old log building at night can be seen across the lake in the town, intensified as if it were shining through a magnifying glass.

The November clouds part and moonlight illuminates the rear porch of the Rainwater barn. The back door opens, and gray-haired Gabriel Rainwater exits. He is a pleasant-looking, strong-featured fellow of indeterminant age. He wears blue jeans, a blue denim shirt, and a Native American style coat of many colors, mostly shades of blue. He carries an old-fashioned, cracked black leather doctor's bag. The smell of piñon pine follows him as he walks.

Gabriel is the town's only physician. He's about to row across the lake with the help of his twelve-year-old grandson to make a house call. They are on their way to see Jane James, a seriously ill young woman. Jane is the owner of the Blue Moon Inn, a tourist lodge on the water's edge. Dr. Rainwater is answering an urgent call from Cleo Newday, the lady who owns the Newday Boat Marina next door to the inn. Jane and Cleo are best friends. Gabriel is fighting to save Jane's life, but he fears he is losing the battle.

The old doctor is followed from the rear barn door by his grandson, Chris, a boy with a look of strength about him common to youngsters reared in these mountains, who grow up with boat paddles, snow shovels, and wood-splitting axes in their hands. The tools vary with the season, but the strenuous nature of their lives does not. These are sturdy boys, not easily dissuaded by the elements or deterred by the job at hand. They do their duty, as they have been taught to see it. And they are fiercely loyal to their families; Chris more so than most. Gabriel passes Chris his heavy doctor's bag and starts down the steps toward the dock. Chris carries the bag in both arms and follows his grandfather.

A moment later, a big-headed, thick-necked black English Labrador noses out the barn door. The self-assured canine spots Chris ahead of him on the steps and moves to overtake him. Standing on his skinny bird legs atop the dog's big back is a fat-bodied black-and-white Australian jaybird, also known as a camp robber because of his species' propensity for stealing food left unattended. This bird is particularly prone to snatching any bit of unguarded blueberry muffin he happens to spy, spearing and carrying it aloft on the point of his long beak.

The dog and his avian passenger catch up to Chris and push by him on the stone steps. "Slow down, you two," Chris says as they crowd him. "This isn't a race." But then he picks up his pace, moves past the pushy dog and bird, and arrives at the dock just behind his grandfather.

The old doctor unties and steps into the largest canoe. "I'll take my bag now, Chris."

The boy hands it to him. "How is Amanda's mother doing, Grandfather?

"Not well, Chris."

"She's going to be okay, isn't she?"

"We'll just have to see, won't we?"

Chris goes with his grandfather on most of his house calls, especially those that come in the middle of the night like tonight. Gabriel, the big dog, and the strange looking bird riding on the canine's back are the only family Chris has. In the 1980s, when he was four, a big snow avalanche on Shadow

Mountain damaged much of the town of Good Bear Lake and killed several residents, including both of Chris's parents, John and Linda Rainwater.

Chris turns and speaks to the jaybird: "Shoo, get up there and guide us across."

The jaybird opens his broad wings into the stiffening late fall breeze and is lifted away. Chris starts to step into the canoe but is edged aside by the big dog.

"Francis, your manners are bad, even for a dog." Chris gives the big lab a dirty look. The lab gives it right back and settles in between the canoe's two seats.

Chris gets into the boat, and Gabriel hands him a paddle. Francis grabs Chris's paddle blade in his mouth and hangs on.

"Knock it off, you two," Gabriel says. "We have important work to do."

Chris and Francis drop their heads and comply. Neither wants to do anything of which Gabriel would disapprove. Dr. Rainwater is the mayor of their town and, more importantly, the head ranger of the local chapter of the Federated Union of Rangers. He is held in high esteem by all, especially by Chris, his grandson, and Francis, his dog, who love him more than their own lives.

"Let's get going, Chris," Gabriel adds.

Chris pushes off, and he and Gabriel begin to paddle toward the far shore.

Moonlight shows them the way across the choppy, blue-black water. Shoo flies above them, dropping down occasionally to highlight the most direct route. Gabriel and Chris wave their approval to the swooping jaybird between paddle strokes. Shoo is more than just their eyes in the sky. As a member of the Rainwater family, he plays an important part in fulfilling their mission on Rainwater Island.

This trip is one the Rainwaters often make several times

each day, but the bird's help is much appreciated in the dark of night, especially with the wind picking up and the weather changing for the worse. It isn't long before they see a yellow light shining through the leafless aspen stand that surrounds the Blue Moon Inn. Gabriel and Chris turn the nose of their small craft in toward shore and paddle in concert, moving swiftly.

Chapter 2

Tiny, Intense Blue Light

Blue Moon Inn

The two-story split log tourist lodge sits not far from the water's edge. The structure is old, though not as old as the Rainwater house and barn. Yet, like the Rainwater compound, the Blue Moon Inn has survived many a rugged Rocky Mountain winter. And the same great avalanche that killed Chris's parents in the '80s, that also had killed Cleo Newday's husband, Bill.

Gabriel and Chris moor their small craft at the cove dock next to the canoe Amanda, Jane James's daughter, uses when she and Chris go out on the lake together. Along with Francis, they disembark and take the short single-track trail that leads through the stand of leaf-vacant aspens to the inn.

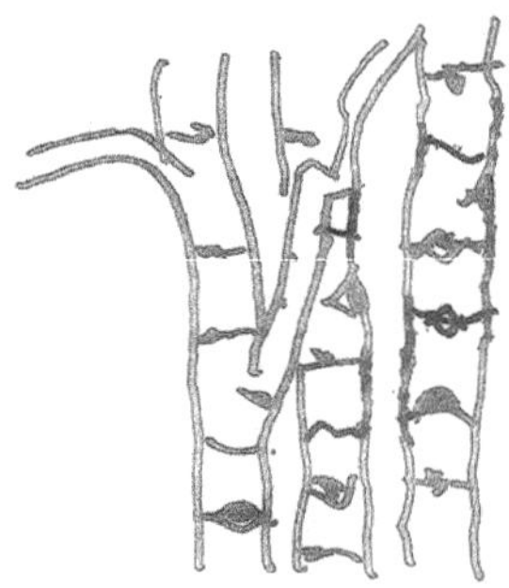

The tall trees that flank the forest path are one under the skin of the volcanic ground—one family, one being, one life. What affects one affects all. This night, the autumn-stripped trees watch with their dark winter eyes as the grandfather leads the grandson and his dog on a mission of mercy. Soon the trio reaches the clearing and can see the lamp light coming from the front second-floor window of the otherwise dark log structure ahead.

Inside, a woman in her late thirties, Jane James, lies in her bed, dressed in a high-collared woolen sweater. Her breathing is labored, and her skin, a sallow gray in the minimal light provided by the small bedside lamp with tassels on the shade and a porcelain butterfly on its belly. She has double pneumonia and is not responding to the medications Gabriel has been giving her. The doctor is not hopeful about her recovery unless she turns the corner very soon.

Outside, Gabriel, Chris, and Francis pass the weather-beaten Blue Moon Inn sign creaking in the stiff breeze. A second later, Shoo, the camp robber bird, lands on the sign, digs his jaybird's talons into the wood, and hangs on, blown by a stout Colorado wind.

Watching them from the front porch of the inn is Cleo Newday, the ruddy-cheeked mountain woman who made the phone call to Gabriel earlier. If Cleo were made to hold coffee, she would have been a hand-thrown pottery mug, strong with a comfortable handle. She is a hardy woman and not easy to chip. Standing on the porch next to her is her son, Jack, who has a camera case hanging from a strap around his neck and a look of concern on his boyish face. Chris and Jack share many things: their ages, their hardy mountain lifestyles, and the common experience of having lost a parent. Yet, they are not good friends. In fact, they are not friends at all.

Gabriel immediately goes up the steps as Amanda, Jane James's teary-eyed eleven-year-old daughter, exits the front door. She has her mother's porcelainlike skin and high red-apple cheeks but lacks her mother's innate physical brittleness. Amanda's pretty face is haloed by auburn hair, thick and lustrous. It falls straight until her shoulders, where the ends turn up in natural curls.

Chris looks up at her from below as if she were a miracle of nature. He is hopelessly smitten, though he has no idea what smitten means, and he has been since the first time he saw her. Gabriel and Francis make matters worse by remarking that Amanda feels the same way about him.

It's two in the morning and cold outside. Chris is tired and sleepy, yet seeing Amanda makes him feel immediately better—warm inside and just plain old good all over. It's an unexplainable feeling that makes no sense to Chris. Like being smitten, he has no earthly idea where it comes from or what it means. Francis insists it's a simple matter of love at first sight and that Chris might as well get used to the fact that he's been stuck. Love at first sight is what it is, and it's a permanent condition. Francis has told him this more than once. But Chris resists Francis's conclusion because, since losing his parents, he no longer believes in love.

"How's Jane doing?" Gabriel asks Cleo.

Cleo bows her head. "She's been getting steadily worse all night."

The old doctor reaches for Amanda and holds her to him. "One way or another, my little love," he whispers into her cold ear. "I'm here to take care of your sweet mother."

Amanda turns her face up to look at him. "Thank you, Dr. Rainwater."

Cleo touches Amanda's arm. "Better wait outside with the boys, dear."

Gabriel kisses Amanda's forehead and follows Cleo inside the inn. Jack goes down the porch steps as Chris comes up. The boys avoid each other's gaze.

Chris joins Amanda on the porch. They look together toward Rainwater Island and then at each other but say nothing. Amanda takes a deep breath and sits on the top step. Chris sits beside her. At the bottom of the stairs, Jack stands beside

Francis. When he tries to pet the big dog, Francis ducks his head and moves away.

Inside the inn, Cleo and Gabriel climb the steps and enter Jane's bedroom. Gabriel places his bag on the table by the window that looks out over the lake. As he opens the bag, he sees a tiny intense blue light emanating from their barn on the island. He hesitates for a moment as the light grows larger and stronger. He closes his bag and moves to Jane's bedside.

"What is it, Gabriel?" Cleo asks.

"Better leave us alone, Cleo," Gabriel replies, and Cleo slips out the door.

On the front porch, Chris starts to reach for Amanda's hand and then remembers he can't offer his to her. He knows what would happen if she really did love him and willingly took it. The same thing that had happened to his father's brother, Uncle William, who had converted, become human, so he could marry a human woman many years before. Chris pulls his hand suddenly back. Surprised and hurt, Amanda jumps to her feet.

Chris knows Amanda's mother is deathly ill, and now her best friend has rejected her. He understands how she must feel as she charges down the steps and heads for the path that leads to the lake. He regrets what he has done, has had to do, but for him, being who he is, there was no other option. Followed by Francis, he runs after Amanda and stops by the sign where Shoo is still swinging back and forth in the November breeze. He can't risk letting Amanda go out on the lake alone in the dark, especially not in this weather.

"Stay with Amanda, Shoo," he says to the jaybird.

Shoo releases his wind-blown perch and flies away. Chris and Francis follow Amanda down the slender single trail.

Jack catches up. "Hey, where's Amanda going?"

"Away from me," Chris says.

When she reaches the cove dock, Amanda steps into her canoe, pushes out, and paddles into the chilled night. Shoo hovers overhead in the dark. Chris and Francis arrive and step into their own boat.

"You guys, wait up!" Jack shouts and climbs into Chris's canoe. He picks up a paddle, and they follow Amanda's canoe onto the wind-tossed lake.

It begins to snow, fat flakes glistening in the sudden flood of blue light coming from the island. The face of the yellow moon above the rough water has been totally washed in blue.

In the bedroom on the second floor of the inn, the blue light has reached the window and pours in and onto the dying Jane James. It moves from the foot of her bed, over her handmade patchwork quilt, until it finds Jane's peaceful face. She opens her eyes weakly and smiles. Then she closes them for the last time and is gone.

Standing beside the bed, Gabriel changes from his human form into a tall, furry creature most people would call Bigfoot. Gabriel and others of his kind prefer the name Ranger but over time have become inured to the thousand-year-old misnomer. They have learned to even welcome its usage, which disguises the real purpose of their existence and protects their true identities.

Anything but scary, Gabriel's comforting demeanor and the resolve in his expression are unchanged from his human form and easily recognizable. He extends his hairy hand toward Jane's thin white-skinned one. Bathed in blue light, Jane's spirit leaves her body, takes Bigfoot Gabriel's powerful hand, and rises from the bed. Together, they enter the cloud of blue that now fills the room and disappear out the window in a puff, as if they were sucked out by a powerful unseen vacuum.

Chapter 3

Large, Obscure Swimmer

Good Bear Lake

Amanda paddles hard, struggling against the increasing waves. Her canoe hits a swell, and she's tossed into the dark, freezing water. As Chris and Jack paddle frantically toward her empty boat, she surfaces, gasping for air.

Jack sees her first. "Chris, there she is!" he shouts as Amanda drops beneath the surface once again.

Chris knows Amanda will not survive in the cold water for long, and neither would he, not in his human form. He also knows there is a way to save her. Yet that would mean certain exposure with Jack in the boat as a witness. But this is his Amanda, and Chris is determined to save her no matter what the risk might be to him. He stands in the canoe and dives in after her. Before he enters the water, he shapeshifts into his own Bigfoot form. It is clearly much younger than Gabriel's yet, like his grandfather's manifestation, benign and quite recognizable as the young Chris. Jack is shocked speechless. He fumbles, as he takes his camera from its case.

Underwater, young Bigfoot Chris can see the drowning Amanda losing consciousness as she sinks. He takes strong strokes toward her with his muscular arms—a large, obscure swimmer—grabs Amanda by her shoulders, and pulls her toward the blue-lit surface above.

From inside Chris's canoe, Jack can clearly see young Bigfoot Chris pushing the semi-conscious Amanda aboard her boat. He takes picture after picture as fast as he can punch the camera button. As Amanda regains momentary consciousness, she catches a glimpse of young Bigfoot Chris in the light from Jack's camera flash. Her eyes close.

Dipping below the surface of the water, Chris changes back into his human form and then pulls himself into Amanda's canoe. He covers the shivering Amanda with his jacket and begins to paddle toward shore. Jack puts his camera in its case and sets it aside. Then he picks up a paddle and follows them toward the cove.

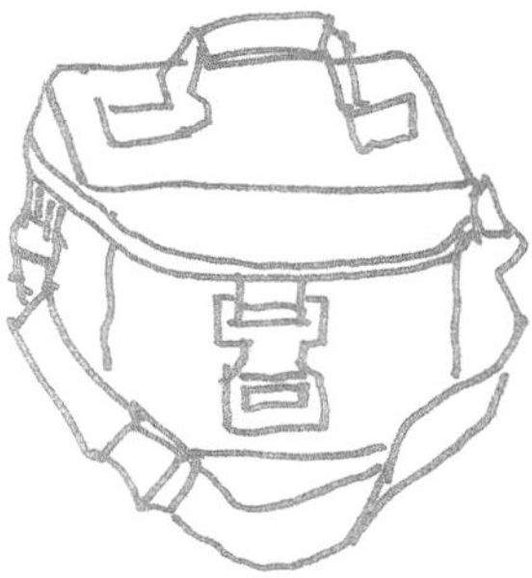

As they near the dock, unseen by Jack, Francis takes the strap of Jack's camera case in his mouth and lowers it into the dark water. The snow continues to fall as the mass of blue light recedes toward Rainwater Island, and the photographic evidence of Chris's life-altering rescue disappears below the surface of the lake.

Chapter 4

Piñon Pine and a Small Puppy

Rainwater Island

Across the lake, Bigfoot Gabriel is escorting Jane James's spirit to the island inside a cloud of blue light in the middle of a full-blown, big-faced blue moon event. The usual explanation of a blue moon concludes that its cause is both scientific and predictable, but the truth is, it is neither. A blue moon is a spiritual, not a scientific, happening. It occurs in an unscheduled fashion when a human spirit is coming into or going out of this world, like Jane James's is doing tonight.

It's a big job and requires a great deal of love. As it turns out, the color of love is blue. When the moon is blue, it is reflecting a world that has suddenly been filled with love. There is no sadness for Jane's spirit this night, since love is never sad. She travels with Bigfoot Gabriel in an azure cascade toward Rainwater Island. Above the ancient barn, they enter a whirling vortex of blue and are pulled down, as if they were made of metal and the barn were a powerful magnet.

Once inside the yawning space, blue light precedes Bigfoot Gabriel and Jane James's spirit as they move toward the steps leading to the level below. They are surrounded by animals: elk, bighorn sheep, a cougar, a kite of little foxes, a black bear, and—fluttering down from the upper limbs of the Douglas fir that grows in the middle of the dark barn—a snow goose, a red-tailed hawk, and a great horned owl.

Like an honor guard, the animals disperse and form lines on either side of the staircase so that Bigfoot Gabriel and Jane James's spirit might enter. Once inside, Bigfoot Gabriel and Jane James's spirit follow the light to the bottom of the steps. Bigfoot Gabriel places his right hand flat against the door at the bottom. It immediately opens. He waits as the blue light returns in a *whoosh* to its place of origin.

There are many such places throughout the world designated as portals by the Federated Union of Rangers, each with its own characteristics. The portal in the Rainwater barn at Good Bear Lake smells like a piñon pine forest after a rain, and the only sound heard inside is the low-pitched guttural expression of joy made by a small puppy when it has located its mother. It's purposefully a comforting place, a soft place, a place that Gabriel, as head ranger of this division of the federation, has served his entire life. The purpose of each portal, however, is the same worldwide, to assist human spirits in transit. And inside each portal, the air is always the same color: blue, the color of love.

Bigfoot Gabriel leads Jane James's spirit in by the hand to meet her spirit guides, people from her life who have proceeded her, people whom she has loved and who have loved her. They await her spirit on the inside and will lead it on its final journey home.

After a time, Bigfoot Gabriel returns alone, closes the door, which remains faintly blue for another moment, shapeshifts into his human form, and climbs the steps to the barn, where he finds the animals have reverted to their inanimate forms. They are now carved wooden replicas of their animate selves, including the three big birds, who are perched again on their high limbs.

Gabriel goes to the rear of the barn, slips off his multicolored jacket, hangs it on a hook, and then enters his woodworking shop. He sits at his table, choses a chisel and a mallet, and begins to work on his latest project.

Chapter 5

Vote Being Tied

Good Bear Lake City Hall, Friday, November 2018

Much has changed in the twenty years since the death of Jane James and Amanda's move to Denver to live with her father. During that time, Chris, who is still sturdy and steady as a rock, has completed his medical training and returned to Good Bear Lake. He lives on the island and is taking his grandfather's place as the town's physician. Retired, Gabriel now spends much of his time in his woodworking shop, making things for people who need them and charging no one.

Jack Newday helps his mother, Cleo, who is busy as ever running their boat marina. He is also the captain of the local volunteer fire department, a job he was awarded because he and his mother own the only powerboat allowed on the lake. Jack is still convinced that Chris is Bigfoot, and he devotes much of his spare time and energy trying to expose him to the Good Bear Lake community. So far, to no avail.

However, many things have remained the same. Francis the dog is still pushy and thinks he knows it all, and Shoo the jaybird is redundant, generally tardy everywhere he goes, and perpetually hungry, especially for blueberry muffins. The Rainwater family still takes care of that "old as time" barn on Rainwater Island, with its intermittently animating herd of wooden animals, its living Douglas fir tree, and the blue air–filled, piñon pine–smelling, puppy-sounding basement. Gabriel is still the town mayor, as he has been for forty years. And Good Bear Lake remains a small town that looks and acts pretty much the same as it did the day Amanda left those twenty years ago.

This morning, citizens walk across Elk Avenue onto the blue grass lawn of the town's city square. They come from all directions, heading toward the steps of the Colorado red sandstone city hall building, to attend the monthly Friday morning town council meeting. Though it is a regularly scheduled meeting, there is nothing regular about today's docket. Today the water issue will be voted up or down. The outcome of the vote will determine if the town will allow the Denver Water Authority to purchase more water from their lake or not. Local opinions are divided.

The Colorado Water Court has left it up to the Good Bear Lake town council to decide yea or nay. A nay vote will require no action, while a yea vote will require the town to raise the level of the lake from Shadow Mountain Reservoir. Raising the water level means the town would have to condemn two waterfront properties, the Newday Marina and the Blue Moon Inn, as well as Rainwater Island in the middle of the lake. Everyone knows the vote will be close, and the stakes are high, especially for the Rainwaters, who could lose their ancestral family home. And their barn.

The council meeting room on the second floor of city hall is packed. Chris sits at one end of the first row. Jack is seated on the other. Every so often, Jack leans forward, looks in Chris's direction, frowns, and then leans back. There has been no love lost between the two over the years. Jack is strongly in favor of a yes vote because he believes if the island goes under water, it will flush Bigfoot, whom he believes to be Chris, out into the open. Chris, of course, is against anything that will endanger his family's island, especially the barn and the portal beneath it.

The city council members sit at a long table at the front of the large room. A name card stands in front of each. On one side, Mayor Rainwater is joined by the short, dark-skinned Sheriff Bob Big Sky and the extremely kind but somewhat rotund Rev. Dinky Round Rock, the minister of the All Are Welcome Church. The council members on Gabriel's side of the table support a no vote.

On the other side of the gray vinyl-topped table are the three council members in favor of the water sale: the very baldheaded Gus Cobb, the local representative of the Denver Water Authority; the tall, slender, long-necked Tom Throttle, the editor of the *Good Bear Lake News* and the president of the chamber of commerce; and the somewhat chunky but sweet-faced Becky Proudlow, the owner of Proudlow Realty. Tom and Becky like each other but, to date, have done nothing about it.

By herself at the far end of the table, and politically somewhere between the two sides, sits Cleo Newday, still an unchipped pottery mug of a mountain woman and the owner of the Newday Marina. Everyone in the big room watches Cleo, knowing that she likely will be the swing vote. The yes folks keep the pressure on Cleo.

"It'd be a good thing for the town, Cleo," Gus says, "progress-wise."

"It'd be a big bonus for local businesses, Cleo," Becky adds, "economy-wise."

"It'd be a huge perk for our regional image, Cleo," Tom concludes, the Adam's apple in his long neck rising and falling, "chamber-of-commerce-wise."

Outside above Elk Avenue, Shoo, the black jaybird, passes over the Victorian-style wooden buildings with colorful painted-glass front windows. He occasionally drops to street level looking for unattended sources of food. He circles the Corner Cupboard Café hoping for a shot at one of Ruthie Firth's famous blueberry muffins, invariably moist and tasty, but soon gives up and flies low by Summertime Hardware, looking for a sample of Clara Summertime's banana nut bread. Even though her baking tends to be a bit on the dry side, it's still any port in a storm to an empty-bellied camp robber and better than nothing. And yet, zip, nada, no unattended goodies today.

He flies on to city hall, where he spots an open second floor window, takes aim, dives into the council meeting room, and lands on the back of Gus Cobb's chair. He looks at his reflection on the back side of Gus's mirror-shiny baldpate and then hops onto the tabletop. Looking Gus in the eye, he squints. Gus is the opposition, and all bets are off.

"Shoo," Gus says, waving him off.

Despite Gus having unintentionally gotten his name right, Shoo doesn't budge. He squawks a loud jaybird, "*Phooey*," and sits down on his skinny bird butt.

Gabriel snaps his fingers and points at Shoo. Straight away, the big bird jumps up, hops down onto the floor, and hastens underneath the table, his talons clattering on the hard wood.

Gabriel addresses the gathering: "Okay, folks, as most of you already know, we're here today to vote on the motion to allow Denver and their water authority a larger portion of water from our lake. The Colorado Water Court has left it up to us to vote yes or no. A no vote means things would stay as they are."

Chris stands and claps his hands. "Vote no, Cleo!"

"No kibitzing from the audience, please," Gabriel says, pointing at Chris.

"Sorry, Grandfather," Chris says and immediately sits down. Rules are rules.

Gabriel continues, "On the other hand, a yes vote would mean raising the level of our lake to fill the new tunnel the Denver Water Authority is presently building at the water's edge above their old bore." He goes on to explain that this would mean the town would have to condemn the three properties that would be impacted by raising the lake to a higher level.

Jack jumps to his feet, pumps his fist, and shouts, "Whoop, whoop, whoop! Mother, vote yes!"

"That means you too, Jack Newday," Gabriel says. "Sit down."

Jack respectfully takes his seat. "Sorry, Mayor Rainwater."

"Okay, people. We've been discussing this issue for six months now, and as you can see, spirits run high on both sides," Gabriel says, "but now it's time for a vote." He goes over to the chalk board and wipes it clean with a well-dusted old chalk eraser.

Gus focuses on Cleo. "I know we can count on you to do the right thing, Cleo." As Gus speaks, he feels his ankle being pecked. He leans under the table and sees Shoo, who sticks out his tongue and wrinkles his insignificant nose. While sitting up, Gus bumps his bald head against the metal table's edge. Shoo chuckles and scuttles across the wooden floor and out the door on his scratchy bird feet.

Francis waits outside in the hall at the door of the coat closet. Shoo slides into the vacant hallway on his feathered bottom, and Francis flushes him into the empty closet. In the low light, both change their forms, filling the tight space with hairy Bigfoot versions of their still-recognizable English Labrador and Australian jaybird selves.

"What's going on in there?" Bigfoot Francis asks.

"Cleo's getting hammered," Bigfoot Shoo replies.

"Did she say how she's going to vote?"

"Not yet."

Inside the meeting room, Gabriel has made three white chalk marks under yes and two under no. The vote stands at three in favor of the motion to grant Denver's request, Gus, Tom, and Becky, and two against, Rev. Dinky and Sheriff Bob. Only Cleo's vote remains.

"I'm ready now," Cleo says.

Gabriel points with his eraser. "Go ahead."

"No."

Gus is taken aback. "No. Just no?"

Cleo nods. "Yes. Just no."

Tom looks at Becky, who shakes her round head. "Are you sure?" he says.

"I'm sure."

"Are you sure you're sure?" Becky adds.

"Uh-huh. I sure am."

Gabriel marks the board with a squeak. The vote now stands at three to three. Gus, Tom, and Becky deflate. All three know what's coming next.

Gabriel marks a diagonal line across the three no votes. *Squeak.* "The vote being tied three to three, the chair breaks the tie and votes no." Four to three. "Motion fails."

"Cleo, won't you reconsider?" Gus says.

"No!"

Chris jumps to his feet as the room fills with cheers and jeers. Francis and Shoo burst into the room in their usual forms. Francis barks, and Shoo flies around the room squawking. It's a big win for the Rainwaters and for the old barn and its ancient secrets.

Jack gets up and leans across the table to his mother. "Thanks a lot, Mother."

"It's the best thing, son, for all concerned," she says. "One day soon you'll understand."

Jack storms out with a firm, "Phooey."

Gabriel bangs his gavel. "Meeting adjourned."

As the room clears, Chris, Francis, and Shoo come over to Gabriel.

"What happens now, Grandfather?" Chris asks.

Francis barks his agreement with the important question. Shoo follows with a high-pitched jaybird squawk.

Gabriel replies in his usual fashion: "We'll just have to see, then, won't we? But if I were the water authority, I'd send my best man to town now to put pressure on Cleo to change her vote."

But Chris has another question. "Why did Cleo vote no in the first place? She's made Jack really mad at her."

Gabriel coughs and clears his throat. "What Cleo did, she did for all of us, Chris, and that includes Jack."

Chapter 6

What's the Big Hurry?

Blue Moon Inn, Friday next

A week has passed since the council meeting. A car now sits parked in front of the inn, by the old sign, which is dilapidated like the rest of the lodge. The vehicle is covered in dust, suggesting it has come the short way from Denver, the last ten miles of which is a dirt road through a low mountain pass that will close soon for the winter. After the first snowfall, the driver must return to the city using the long way around using the plowed roads or spend the winter in Good Bear Lake.

Inside in the front second floor bedroom of the inn, Jane James's old room, Amanda James, with her high apple–cheeked face surrounded by long auburn hair that still turns up in curls at her shoulders, looks out the window at Rainwater Island. She says to herself with a hint of sadness in her voice, "I wonder if you're still there, Chris, or have you moved on too?" After a quiet moment, she turns to her mother's old bed, half of which rests on the floor, and shakes her auburn hair. She opens her suitcase and removes a jacket with letters embroidered over the pocket—DWA, for Denver Water Authority.

She tries it on and then moves to an ancient wooden wardrobe, opens the creaky door, and finds her mother's old woolen sweater hanging inside.

"Best not to let the whole town know why I'm here or who I'm working for just yet," she says.

After removing the DWA jacket and hanging it over her mother's sweater, she closes the warped wooden door, leaving it slightly ajar. She then clicks off the small bedside lamp with the tasseled shade and the porcelain butterfly on its belly and goes out of the room and down the stairs, which lead to the inn's great room.

At the bottom of the rustic staircase with its Gabriel-carved balusters, Amanda passes through the gathering room with its enormous red-stone fireplace, the dining room with its ponderous deer-antler chandelier, and the kitchen with its footed cast-iron wood-burning stove. All three are sheltered beneath a single tall ceiling, a great room spanned by four matching wooden trusses. The inn is as beautiful as ever. The bones of the expansive space are still better than good, but the years have taken their toll. Chairs with broken legs have been upended. The dining table lies on its back on the filthy hand-hewn wooden floorboards. The old hand-blown glass double-hung windows are intact but have broken pull cords and are stuck shut and mud-covered, rendering the outside hardly visible. The window coverings have fallen and heaped themselves into piles on the floor. The iron stove's door is off its hinges and lying on the floor, and the surfaces of the local granite kitchen countertops are finger-deep in long-undisturbed Colorado dust.

Yet, beneath the remains of time blanketing the inn are the best eleven years of Amanda's life, memories of her mother, of

Chris, and of Gabriel, Chris's grandfather, really, her grandfather too, the only one she has ever known. Amanda remembers how much she and her mother had loved this old place and the people who had moved in and out of their lives here. But that portion of Amanda has long since been put aside. Things are different now, no matter how she had once felt about the inn. Or her safe-feeling memories of this little town or its safe-feeling people. Especially, her special young friend, Chris Rainwater.

She exits the front door, the handmade Gabriel-carved relic with the leaf-barren, black-eyed aspen trees on its outer surface. She recalls the day Gabriel hung the door, a special door, Gabriel had promised, that would always recall the love that lived in this house. It was a present from her father to her mother on Jane's thirtieth birthday, when Amanda was still surrounded by love, five years before her parents divorced and six before her mother died and Amanda went to Denver to live with her successful, hard-driving businessman father. Before the aspens on her mother's door closed their dark eyes and lost their wooden leaves. Before the special door was locked and forgotten, along with the love left inside.

Stepping onto the front porch, Amanda sits on the top step, the same step where she and Chris sat side by side twenty years before, the night she lost her mother. She had been in tears then and is beginning to be so again. Chris had held out his hand to comfort her and then withdrew it suddenly. She feels for a moment how she felt then, abandoned by her mother and then by her best friend, Chris. She clears her throat, stands, and wipes the unexpected moisture from her reddening cheeks. She hasn't cried in years, not since her mother died. Why now? Silly. Especially given the reason she was in town.

"Amanda?" the ruddy-faced, pottery mug of a mountain woman standing on the lawn below says.

Amanda focuses. "Cleo Newday. Is that you?"

"It is. I saw your headlights pull up last night, and when I saw that auburn hair of yours on the porch just now, I knew exactly who it was."

"Great to see you, Cleo. You're just who I was hoping to run into today." Which is entirely true. Cleo and her vote are the issue of the day.

"What brought you to town after all this time, girl?"

"I'm here to sell the inn." Which is only partially true. The rest of the story is that Amanda works as the chief trouble-shooter for the Denver Water Authority. She's Gabriel's "best man," the person the DWA has sent to Good Bear Lake to get Cleo to change her vote on the water issue. If Amanda can get the job done quickly, it will be a real feather in her cooperate cap and mean a big bonus for her wallet.

"Your mother loved this old place," Cleo says.

"I was just thinking that myself. I guess we both did," Amanda replies and starts down the steps, "but that was a long time ago."

Getting rid of the old inn should help her shed some of these memories, memories that could still make her cry. But it's time, as her father would say, to put those thoughts aside and turn to the issue at hand: getting Cleo to change her vote from a no to a yes. Memories are of the long ago, the gone by, he likes to say, while business is of the now.

"I heard yesterday at the gas station in town that you had voted against condemnation of the inn and your marina at last week's city council meeting," Amanda says.

"I did, yes."

"But why? Aren't you tired of renting rowboats to the tourists?"

"Not really, no, and it's not even that. It's what condemnation would do to Rainwater Island that's stopping me."

"Why is that?"

"Because the island is as much a part of our lake as the water itself."

Amanda arrives at the bottom of the steps. "Sounds a bit sentimental."

Cleo looks across the lake to the island. "It does, I know. And it is, but there's more to it than that."

Amanda stands beside Cleo in silence. There is more to it than that. After several seconds, she sniffs and pinches her wet nose. "Do the Rainwaters still live over there?"

"They do. Chris moved back in with his grandfather after his medical training was completed a couple of years ago. Gabriel has retired, and Chris is the town doctor now. He's about to marry his nurse, Lulu Big Sky."

"I remember Lulu. When's the wedding?"

"Tomorrow."

"How long have they been engaged?"

"Since last Saturday."

"Six days? What's the big hurry?"

So soon. Amanda feels an unexplained tug. Why should she care that a man she hasn't seen in twenty years is getting married? They were just kids when they last saw each other. It's not like they were in love. Besides, she doesn't much believe in love any longer. She had loved her mother and that had not worked out so well for either of them.

"Listen, we're having Chris and Lulu's rehearsal dinner at our marina tonight. Why don't you come by? I know everyone would enjoy seeing you. You and I could put our heads together and have ourselves a nice little chat about this condemnation issue."

"How about having that chat right now?" No time like

the present to get the job done, is Amanda's father's absolute favorite.

"Love to, except I've got a walking tour to lead downtown that starts in five minutes. It's Bigfoot Days Festival time again, and I'm on the committee."

"As I remember, you and Mother were always on some committee or other."

"We did hang our share of crepe paper, didn't we? She was such a lovely woman and my very best friend."

"And you were hers. Okay, I'll be there." It would be as good a place as any to get Cleo by herself and, maybe, to get her past this sentimental Rainwater Island hogwash. She sniffs again and again pinches her moistening nose. More than silly. Hopefully she'll be able to close the deal in one day, which would be excellent work even by her father's standards.

"See you next door at six, then," Cleo says and leaves Amanda alone.

Amanda looks across the lake at the island. Chris had pulled her out of the water the night her mother died and saved her life. She did remember being more than his friend, of having liked him, and yet, it was a schoolgirl crush sort of thing at the most. Right?

But why? she thought, after knowing each other their whole lives, would Chris and Lulu Big Sky suddenly decide to get married after an engagement of less than a week? But it is none of her concern. Right now, she has a bigger fish to fry, and that fish is Cleo Newday. Still, she feels a second unexpected pang and suddenly unexplainably wishes she could see Chris again.

Chapter 7

Better, Warm, and Good

Rainwater Island, Friday

Chris leaves the house wearing a Bigfoot costume, with the headpiece tucked under his arm. Francis is with him, and Shoo is riding on Francis's back. Chris looks at the lake. The morning sun is at his back and shining across the water and onto the inn, which glows along the dark shore like a summertime forest lit by a swarm of fireflies. He thinks about the inn, its owner, her auburn-haired daughter, and that early morning visit with his grandfather twenty years ago, and he wishes he could see Amanda again so he could tell her how sorry he is for what happened. Yet, even now, especially now, he wouldn't be able explain to her what had forced him to withdraw his hand. Or that he still misses her. Now there is the matter of his wedding to Lulu tomorrow. This is his life now, Lulu and the portal, not Amanda and the inn. He is who he is, and he has no other option.

This moment of reflection is not lost on Francis. He has seen Chris stop and look at the inn like this often through the years. Wishful, is how he has described Chris's expression during these quiet moments. Long ago, Francis decided that Chris was thinking about Amanda. And now he is doing it again, the day before his wedding to Lulu Big Sky. Wishful is exactly the right word. But wishing is not going to be enough. There are only thirty-six hours left before the "I dos" get said.

Chris focuses. "C'mon, you guys," he says, starting down the porch steps. "We need to check on Gabriel before we head to town."

The threesome enters the dark barn. There's a chill in the air, and the space is all but vacant. With no farm equipment, no tools, no tractor, and no wagon, the purpose of this place is clearly not farming. The lightless interior suggests a cave and is not a fitting home for living creatures. With no sacks of feed or bales of hay, the sawdust-covered floor is instead inhabited by a menagerie of life-sized wooden animals: an elk, a cougar, a kite of red baby foxes, a black bear, and several bighorn sheep. Despite the lack of light, a Douglas fir thrives in the dank. Above, on the highest limbs of the fir, are perched a wooden snow goose, a wooden red-tailed hawk, and a wooden great horned owl—Honk, Red, and Who. Who, the owl, is senior, and it's his job to keep watch over this place and permit only a Rainwater or someone accompanied by a Rainwater to pass. The woodland creatures, high and low, were carved by Gabriel and then painted in such detail that each looks as if they could walk, run, or fly off on their own at any moment.

Besides the entry from the back porch, there are two other doors in the barn. One leads to the stairs down to the portal and the second, to Gabriel's workshop. Chris, Francis, and Shoo walk through the inanimate assemblage of wooden animals and by the Douglas fir. Chris waves up at Who, who waves back.

"Is he in there?" Chris shouts up at the big owl.

Who animates briefly, nods his head, yes, and points with his wing feathers.

Francis and Shoo follow Chris into the open door of

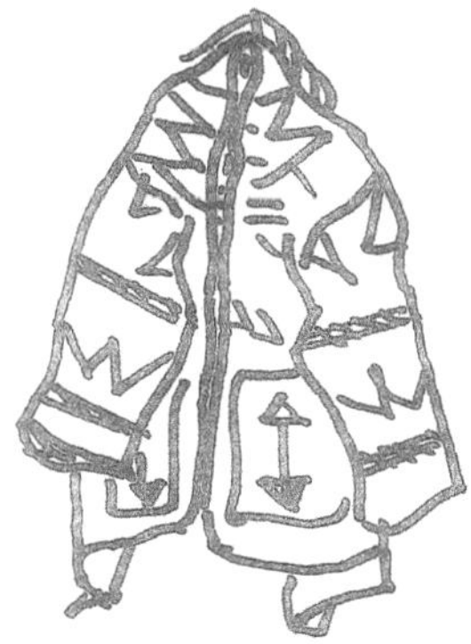

Gabriel's shop. The big room is filled with woodworking paraphernalia, and the air, heavy with dust from Gabriel's power sander. Gabriel sits at his workbench, wearing his favorite old multicolored, mostly blue, coat.

He's working on his latest project: a sign that portrays a two-story log house with a big-faced moon peeking over the mountain behind it. The name plate at the bottom has yet to be carved. The old man's powerful hands move in skillful concert. He wears a wide leather band on his thick right wrist that shows two hands coming together in a firm clasp; one hand is human and the other, not so much.

Chris hesitates at the door and watches his grandfather work, something he always has enjoyed doing. Gabriel is a modest man who doesn't like to talk about himself, especially not about his health, which has for a long time been on the decline. He has been the head ranger at Good Bear Lake for a hundred and fifty years, but his time here is nearing its end. The Rainwaters have watched over this island, its secrets, and its contents for as long as humans have lived around the lake. Chris knows it will fall to him soon, as the last living Rainwater, to take over the job of head ranger when Gabriel is no longer able to serve. Marriage to Lulu Big Sky, the daughter of Bob Big Sky, the president of the local ranger board of directors, will reinforce Chris's position as the new head ranger when the time comes. That he and Lulu don't love each other is true, but then Chris doesn't believe in love as much as he does in those other more important considerations.

Chris, Francis, and Shoo enter the shop just as Gabriel coughs loudly.

"Grandfather!" Chris shouts.

Gabriel raises his visor and switches off the power sander. "What is it?"

"It's way too dusty in here for your lungs."

"My lungs are just fine. I need to finish this sign, and hand-sanding takes too long."

"The boys and I are going in early this morning. Bob Big Sky wants me to stop by the hall before the office to talk about the wedding."

Gabriel shakes his head. "Let me ask you this? How does Lulu make you feel when you see her?"

"Okay, I guess."

"Just okay? Not better, warm, and good?"

"Not really. No."

Gabriel lowers his visor and turns on the sander. "I thought not."

"Grandfather!" Chris shouts again.

"Now what?" Gabriel asks, cutting off the power to his sander.

"You don't believe I love Lulu, do you?"

Francis and Shoo look up at Chris and shake their heads in unison. No, they absolutely don't. No how. No way.

"It's not what I believe, Chris. It's what you believe that counts."

"I believe that love doesn't matter right now."

"Love always matters."

"Not for me."

"We'll just have to see then, won't we?"

Francis nods, agreeing with Gabriel. Whenever Gabriel uses that phrase, he is trying to make someone think. Today's lesson is directed at Chris. It's Gabriel's universal truth: love always matters.

Chris feels Gabriel must know the position he is in and the responsibility that will be his before long. He will have to talk of this again with his grandfather soon, but right now he needs to get to the hall before his office opens.

"Okay, got to go," he says to Gabriel, who again lowers his visor, turns on his sander, and resumes his work.

Shoo flies out the open window, and Chris and Francis retreat into the barn. Chris stops in the middle of the wooden animals.

"Keep your eyes on Gabriel today, you guys."

He slaps the tree trunk and hollers at the birds, singling out the great horned owl.

"Who. Get Grandfather out of that dusty old workshop and into bed for some rest as soon as you can. And get bear or somebody toothy to help you keep him there."

The big wooden owl comes alive. Will do, he salutes. Then he again falls still.

Chris puts on his costume's headpiece, and he and Francis exit the barn and start down the steps to the dock and their canoe.

Chapter 8

Points the Cat

Town of Good Bear Lake, Friday

The sun is shining, and the sky is high-country cloudless blue, but this morning's air has a chill to it, like standing in front of an open refrigerator. Nippy but not out-and-out cold. It's a good portent for the surrounding mountains, which will soon need to store as much snow as possible to fill their summertime rivers and streams. The fall festival has enjoyed perfect weather this year, though a light rain is forecast for Saturday, early afternoon. But the clouds should blow out well before evening.

The forecast for Chris and Lulu's after wedding party in the church's garden is crystal. Clear or not, nothing about this wedding is a comforting thought for Chris, who is still wearing his Bigfoot costume as he steps out of his canoe and onto the town dock at the lake end of Elk Avenue. Francis follows Chris onto the dock, as Shoo flies in and lands on Francis's back.

Chris takes off his headpiece. "Keep your eyes open today, boys, for that Denver Water Authority trouble shooter Gabriel warned us about last week. Lot of strangers in town today for the celebration. He could be any one of them."

Chris leans down with his leash and grabs Francis's collar.

At that moment, Amanda's dust-covered car rolls into view on the short dirt road that leads from the inn into town. A bright-eyed skunk sticks his black head, with a V-shaped white stripe from his tail to the tip of its nose, from under a tarp in Chris's canoe. Francis, Shoo, and the stowed-away skunk see the car at the same time and note its driver. They follow the vehicle with their eyes as Chris busies himself clipping the leash onto Francis's collar and not dropping his costume's oversized headpiece.

"We need to be sharp and stay alert today. Okay, fellows?" Chris reiterates, oblivious to the passing automobile with its high apple–cheeked, auburn-haired female driver with porcelainlike skin and hair that curls up at her shoulders.

Francis and Shoo look at each other in disbelief. The skunk hops onto his short legs and scurries toward town, where the fall Bigfoot festival is in full swing.

Francis tugs Chris under the banner over Elk Avenue, which reads: *Bigfoot Days, November 15–22.* Amanda's car now sits in front of a store up the street with a painted window sign that identifies the building as the Denver Water Authority's Regional Office and Gus Cobb as its director. The architecture of the building is pure Victorian, like the rest of the two-story wooden structures that line both sides of the town's main street—Victorian and overly ornate, as if trying to make up in filigree for what they lack in substance. The paint jobs of their facades are overdone, reminiscent of an old maiden aunt who wears too much makeup. But like the lady herself, the old structures mean well and, for the most part, manage to pull it off.

Across the street ahead, Cleo leads her walking tour. A family of three—a quiet little girl and her mother and father—heads up the group of happy festival goers.

"Why Bigfoot Days, Mrs. Newday?" the mother tourist asks.

"Because Good Bear Lake has had more Bigfoot sightings than any other town in Colorado," Cleo says.

"Why is that?"

"Because we're Bigfoot friendly," she replies and keeps walking.

She points to the giant carved Bigfoot sculpture on the lawn of the city square ahead. As they pass the local newspaper office, the gangly Tom Throttle comes out carrying a stack of weeklies in his long arms and loads them into the coin activated newspaper dispenser out front.

"Morning, folks. Glad to see you in town today," he says to the strolling crowd of tourists. "Hey, Cleo, got a second?"

"For you, Tom, always."

"Then how about changing your vote?"

"Sorry, Tom." Cleo moves quickly by. "Your second's up."

The tourist mother stays with Cleo step for step. "Is there really such a thing as Bigfoot?"

Cleo stops. "As our local Bigfoot expert is fond of saying, 'we'll just have to see then, won't we?'"

"What does that mean exactly?"

"Something different every time."

"I see."

Cleo laughs and moves on. "Then maybe you can explain it to me."

Inside the water authority office, Amanda and Gus discuss why she's here. Gus is pleased that the home office has sent her along. He needs all the help he can get with Cleo, who, he maintains, is as slippery as Coal Creek Alley in snowy February.

Amanda replies that she knows Cleo well and that Cleo was her mother's best friend. "If anybody can get her to change her vote, it's going to be me."

"I hope so. Nobody so far has had any luck."

"She's invited me to Chris and Lulu's rehearsal dinner tonight at the marina. I plan to corner her there and get her turned around."

"Good luck. But you'll find she's a tough nut to turn."

The thing to keep in mind, Amanda reminds Gus, is that the company has already spent a great deal of money on the new second tunnel he's been building over the past year, which is intended to carry the additional DWA water allotment to Denver. Water in this state is liquid gold, and it's up to the two of them to get this council vote reversed and to do so as soon as possible.

"Time is money," she adds, remembering her father.

"I agree, and the new bore is almost complete and will be ready to go soon. We've nearly finished on our side, and the Denver side crew is close as well," Gus replies.

Amanda looks out the front window and sees Cleo and her tour. "Every day that goes by with that new tunnel sitting empty, the company stands to lose a fortune. It's our job to see that the loss is kept to a minimum."

Gus points at Cleo. "There she is now," he says. "For some reason no one quite understands, not even her own son, she resists a proposal that would ensure the sale of her marina to the town at a more than fair price, which would allow her to retire and live comfortably for the rest of her life."

"The hang-up is more than just sentimental is how I heard it from her this morning. She wouldn't say just what the sticking point is, but we can work on getting past that this evening at the rehearsal. Maybe Jack is pressing too hard?" Amanda says. "As I remember, he was very intense as a boy."

"Still is. He says he'll see you this morning at the Corner Cupboard and you all can work on your strategy."

"What does Jack stand to gain from this condemnation?

Just a quick profitable sale of their family's marina or is there something else?"

"He wants Rainwater Island to go underwater because he insists the real Bigfoot lives there, and he wants to flush him out."

"But wouldn't the Rainwater family know about that if it were true?"

"You would think so, yes. Most people in town think Jack's fixation with Bigfoot is way overblown."

Outside on Elk Avenue, Chris's costume headpiece is back in place. Francis is on his leash, and Shoo is on Francis's back. The threesome passes the Summertime Hardware store. The antique establishment smells like leather and oil even on the outside and has a bit of everything on the inside, including two things the supermarket hardware stores don't have: Sam and Clara Summertime. Whatever Sam doesn't know how to repair, Clara can fix. Clara carries more tools in her big purse than most carpenters do on their work belts. The town depends on these two long-time Good Bear Lake residents and their nuts and bolts to keep its old self running smoothly and cost effectively.

Chris waves at the elderly Native American couple inside and then steps back, nearly flattening a furry chipmunk who has just dropped out of the mail slot onto the wooden sidewalk. Chewing a small piece of Clara's crusty banana nut bread and not watching where he is going, the diminutive rodent ends up backing off the wood-planked sidewalk to avoid Chris's Bigfoot costume's big foot. He falls into a puddle in the pothole-pitted street.

"Sorry, Chip," Chris says, lifting the little fellow out of the water-filled hole. He brushes him off and hands him his now soggy piece of pastry. "Clara's banana bread tends to be a bit on the dry side, right, pal?" he says. "Maybe this little dip in the drink will help?"

Chip raises his lip, takes a bite of the wet sweetbread, and scrambles back through the mail slot. He lives here, above the hardware store, doing the little things like the nail and screw sizing, separating the double A batteries from the triples, and keeping the key-making machine oiled and the blank keys on their proper hooks, and so on. A good worker and a good friend to the older Summertime couple, Chip does have the one small problem. He falls a lot, especially when he tries to eat and walk at the same time, which he does frequently and which explains the origin of his Native American name, Chipmunk Who Falls A Lot.

A fire-engine red pickup comes slowly up Elk and passes the fully costumed Chris as he walks along the creaky sidewalk. It's Jack Newday's truck, and Jack is behind the wheel.

Mounted over the rear window is a gun rack, from which hangs a bow and an arrow-filled quiver. Pulling his truck to the curb, Jack watches Chris approaching in his rear-view mirror. He readies his camera and picks up a sleek-bodied cat from the seat beside him. He calls out the window to Chris as he passes, "Hey, Mr. Bigfoot!" He points the cat at Chris.

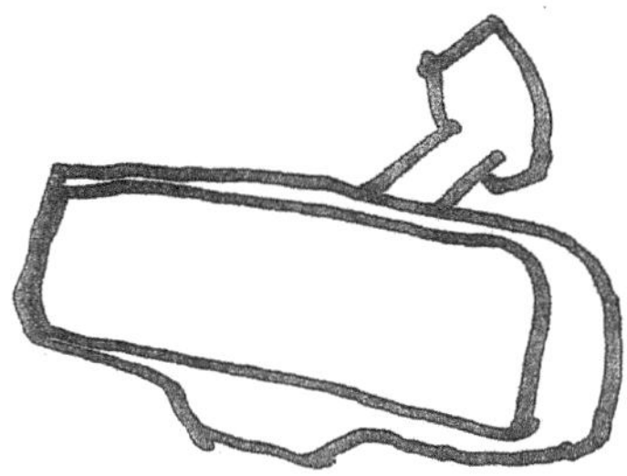

Nothing happens.

Chris removes his headpiece and leans down. "Sorry, Jack, it's only me. Nice cat, though."

"Your days are numbered, Mr. Bigfoot!" Jack shouts out the window.

Chris replaces his headpiece and moves on.

Across the street, Amanda steps out of Gus's office. Once

again Chris fails to see her, but not Francis. He stops. Jack's cat jumps out of the pickup window and runs to Amanda, her collar bell tinkling.

"Goodness, girl," Amanda says to the cat, "I love that little bell."

Francis lunges forward, pulling Chris across the street by his leash and barking as Shoo flies away. Almost knocking Amanda down, Francis eyes the sleek cat with suspicion.

Amanda regains her balance. "Francis? Is that you?" she says to the dog. "That can't be you, not after all this time!"

"Oh, no, that's not Francis," Chris says in a voice muffled by his headpiece. "This dog's name is Frank."

Francis looks up at Chris and smiles. He obviously likes the name. Frank.

"Who exactly am I talking to?" Amanda asks.

Chris removes his headpiece and sets it on the curb. Amanda is surprised.

"Chris, is that you?"

"Yeah, it's me."

"Yeah, it's me," is not the way Francis wants to see Chris begin this conversation. He shakes his head and circles the twosome. The leash tightens around Chris and Amanda's legs and forces them together. That's better. Their knees are almost touching. Definite progress.

"How have you been?" Chris asks Amanda.

"I've been good."

They move closer and closer.

"You look good."

They are now nearly nose to nose.

"I am good."

"That's good." Which is just how Chris is feeling. Better, warm on the inside, and good. The opposite of how he felt when he learned, after the death of her mother, that Amanda had gone to live with her father in Denver. It had been as if a big part of his heart had left with her, much like he'd felt when he lost his mother and his father in the avalanche. She had suddenly gone and now here she is again, just as suddenly. And without a warning either time.

Chris looks at Amanda without speaking. She is as much a miracle of nature as before. More so. The cute young girl has become a beautiful woman. Across the street, the thick-bodied Becky Proudlow comes out of her real estate office and joins Chris, Amanda, and Francis in the street.

"Amanda James. It's Becky Proudlow. What brings you to town after so many years?"

The two women shake hands.

"Good to see you again, Becky. I've come to sell the Blue Moon."

"I'd be happy to sell it for you."

"Thanks, but I'm thinking the town will be buying the property soon."

"Hope so," Becky says and focuses on Chris, who frowns at the two comments. "So, Chris, tomorrow's the big day," she says to him before he can reply to Amanda's prediction.

"What?" Chris replies as he continues to hold onto Amanda, lost in her green eyes. A miracle for sure. Times two.

Amanda breaks the embrace and steps out of the leash. "Cleo told me this morning you were getting married tomorrow. Is that right?"

"Oh, yeah, that's right, I am."

"Cleo says it's to Lulu Big Sky," Amanda adds.

"Your nurse, remember? Pretty girl, long black hair, big brown eyes," Becky says.

"I always liked Lulu," Amanda says.

"Me, too," Chris replies.

"Good thing," Becky affirms.

Outside the hardware store, across the street from Proudlow Realty, the bright-eyed fuzzy black skunk from the canoe and Chip, the hungry chipmunk with the impaired position sense, watch the goings on in the street. The skunk shakes his head and takes off toward Coal Creek Alley behind the Corner Cupboard Café. Chip steps off the curb and falls into the same pothole puddle. He climbs out, shakes off, goes to the front door of the hardware store, and knocks. Clara Summertime opens the door, hands Chip a little blue towel, and ushers him inside.

Becky says goodbye and returns to her office, leaving Chris and Amanda standing in the middle of the street.

"Are you staying at the inn?" Chris asks.

"Yes, but the place is such a mess. Mother's old bed collapsed last night with me on it."

"I'll bet it's your slats. I could stop by later today and have a look if you'd like? Shouldn't be too tough to fix."

"Only if you have the time. I know you'll be busy today."

"No trouble. The inn is on my way home." Besides, he'd like to see her again. Wedding or no wedding.

"See you later this afternoon, then."

"That you will."

Though he knows it can come to nothing, Chris is already looking forward to this afternoon's visit with Amanda. He nearly trips over a frustrated Francis as Amanda heads for the café and her meeting with Jack.

"What's the matter with you?" he asks the big dog, who rolls his eyes, sticks out his long tongue, and makes an odd sound with his canine lips that sounds a lot like, "*Phooey*."

Chapter 9

Francis Rainwater, 1718–1868

Ranger Hall, Friday

Chris and Francis walk across the town square lawn, heading for Ranger Hall. They pass by the wooden Bigfoot standing on the grass. The sculpture stands in a circle of full-bodied Colorado blue spruce. The scene looks like a Rocky Mountain version of England's Stonehenge. Each tree is decorated from top to bottom with blue LED lights that, during the fall festival, come on at six and go off at ten automatically so as not to bother the locals who go to bed early. The Bigfoot in the middle was constructed in sections on the island by Gabriel and then reassembled here for the first fall festival many years ago. The benign-looking giant has his right arm open wide in a welcoming posture and his left raised above his head as if waving hello. His facial features remind many in town of Gabriel, smiling slightly as if he knows something the rest of those who stop to look up at him don't.

On the far side of the lawn, on the corner across from the Corner Cupboard Café, sits Ranger Hall. Like most of the other buildings on Elk Avenue, it's a classic old Victorian, from its decorative porch to the exquisite multicolored paint job of its façade. Lots of blue. The wooden face covers the rustic two-story structure behind it. Like the other roofs on this street, Ranger Hall's is steeply sloped to better shed the high volume of snow in the winter months. The severe inclination also prevents it from collapsing under the snow's weight or leaking because of water backup caused by ice dams that form along its edges.

The rectangular false front rises above the highest gable of the roof behind it and has a painted semicircle at the top that announces the name of the building, Ranger Hall, and below that, three unexplained initials, FUR.

Built off the roof on the side nearest the lake is a viewing platform, much like a widow walk on top of a nineteenth century seaside home, a structural add-on that provided a good view of the ocean. The view from Ranger Hall's high platform is of Good Bear Lake, Rainwater Island, and, particularly, the barn at the rear of the Rainwater house.

Chris and Francis pass through the front door of the hall and enter the high-ceilinged, white-walled foyer, an austere room, empty except for a table at the center with a white wooden box sitting atop it. The lid of the box features a pair of carved clasped hands: the same symbol that appears on Gabriel's leather wristband. Chris removes one of his costume gloves, opens the lid, and places his right hand flat inside the box. The box glows faintly blue, and the door leading to the staircase behind him clicks open.

"Back in fifteen minutes," he says to Francis. "Stay out of trouble."

Leaving his costume gloves and headpiece on the foyer table, Chris starts up the staircase. Portraits hang on the wall side of the stairs, from bottom to top, oil paintings of men holding their right hands over their hearts. Each man wears an identical clasped hands wristband, but each is dressed uniquely, as if each portrait was painted during a different time period. Yet, all the men share the same last name: Rainwater.

The dates below the pictures go way back, many hundreds of years. The next to the last portrait is of Francis Rainwater. The date beneath it reads: 1718–1868. The final portrait is of Chris's grandfather, Gabriel Rainwater, with a single date below: 1868–.

Next to Gabriel is an empty frame with an empty plaque beneath it. It's the space where Chris believes his portrait and dates of service as head ranger will one day hang.

"Bob, it's Chris," Chris shouts as he reaches the landing. Above the landing, the stairs continue up to the door that leads to the roof and the outside viewing platform.

"I'm in the meeting room, Chris," Bob Big Sky shouts back.

Downstairs in the foyer, Francis pushes the front door open with his snout and leaves the hall.

Chapter 10

Buttermilk Pancakes and Two Eggs Over Easy

Corner Cupboard Café, Friday

Catty-corner across Elk is the oldest structure in town, circa 1885. Timewise, it's not in the same league as the Rainwater house and barn, but the rugged building is still old, even for this town. And, like the Blue Moon Inn, the Corner Cupboard Café is one of the few structures that survived the big Shadow Mountain snow avalanche with little to no damage.

The Cupboard is a two-story split log affair with a restaurant downstairs and the living quarters on the second floor for the owners, Ruthie and Lyle Firth, and their three sons. The restaurant's walls are covered with photos of parades, canoe races, weddings, firework displays, and kids, mostly boys, mostly the three small Firths. This morning, the tables are full—breakfast being the café's busiest time of the day—except for an empty table for two by the front window.

Amanda comes in and is ushered to the small window table by Ruthie Firth, the very pregnant waitress, who, along with her pencil-thin husband, Lyle, not only owns but also runs the rustic eatery.

"Coffee?" Ruthie asks Amanda.

Amanda nods and sits, and Ruthie pours her a cup.

"Thanks."

"You're welcome," Ruthie says.

"When are you due?" Amanda asks.

"Today, actually."

"Cutting it a bit close there, aren't you?"

"When you're the mother of three little boys, dearie, close is the best you can hope for."

As he cooks, Lyle reads from the local newspaper to his customers through the serving window: "Get this. Chamber of Commerce President Tom Throttle predicts a quick reversal of the town's position on the Denver Water Authority's request." He stops to spatula up a pancake and then sets a full plate on the ledge for Ruthie to serve.

"Good luck with Cleo on that one, Tom," Ruthie says. She picks up the plate from the counter and delivers it to a heavy-bearded hunter type in the far corner, sitting with three other outdoorsy-looking men. All four are dressed in camouflage brown and green. One wears a cap that reads, *NRA Forever.* Another man's "gimme" hat suggests PETA should go to the devil, or thereabouts.

"Number two, buttermilk pancakes and two eggs over easy, hash browns, and one of Ruthie's famous blueberry muffins," Ruthie says and refills the coffee cups all around.

"Thanks, Ruthie," the man in the NRA booster cap says. "You're the best."

"And the biggest."

The man with the thick beard smiles and digs in as Jack comes in and goes straight to Amanda's table. He carries the cat Amanda met earlier on the street.

"Amanda. Jack Newday."

"Sure, Jack. Good to see you again. Won't you join me for a bite of breakfast, and we can talk? I've already ordered."

Jack sits. "Thanks, but I brought my own." He takes out a package of Twinkies, pops it open, removes one, and pushes the goo-filled cake into his mouth.

"So." Amanda studies Jack's fancy feline. "This is your cat, then?"

With his mouth full, Jack replies, "Yeah. I found her online."

"What's her name?" she asks, sipping her coffee.

Jack stuffs the end of his Twinkie in past his lips with his index finger. "Ebay."

"What kind is she?"

Chewing. "Himalayan."

"Are Himalayans known for anything special?"

Muffled: "Oh, yeah."

Chapter 11

Lineage-Wise

Ranger Hall, Friday

At the center of the meeting room upstairs is a large circular table. In the middle of the table is an inscription that reads in deeply carved letters, *Federated Union of Rangers*, which explains the FUR acronym on the hall's façade.

Bob Big Sky, a stout, dark-skinned Native American man, sits in the large chair at the head of the table, his big-billed western-style sheriff's hat resting on the tabletop in front of him. His straight, coal black hair is pulled back and tied at the nape of his thick neck with a leather strap and left to fall casually in a ponytail that reaches the middle of his back. Bob is the sheriff of Good Bear Lake, a man with a precise, complete look about him. And he is just that, precise and complete. He, however, is not a man. Sheriff Bob is the chairman of the Ranger Hall directorate, the crowd of local ranger portal protectors. And, as chairman of the directors who occupy the ten big chairs around this great table, Bob is second in command to Gabriel in this part of the world. Like Gabriel, Bob is a Bigfoot. He's also Lulu's father.

Chris stands at the window, looking down at the café across the street. He can see Amanda at the table in the front window, sipping coffee and talking with Jack Newday. Maybe they have just run into each other accidentally and are getting reacquainted? And why should he care? But he can't help it. He does.

Looking at Amanda, even at this distance, Chris again feels good. Maybe the inn won't sell quickly and, with the vote having gone against property condemnation, maybe she'll have to stay for a while to sell her mother's old place. Or maybe she'll decide to stay permanently and fix it up, reopen, and run it herself—something he wouldn't mind doing himself. And maybe she'll decide to build a few fishing cabins along the shoreline and rent canoes from Cleo. The makings of a good life, Chris thinks, yet not a life for him, since he is destined to become head ranger one day soon and tomorrow is going to marry Bob's daughter, Lulu. It is a marriage of importance to the entire Ranger Federation. Provenance is a big deal with federation folks, and there can be none better than he and Lulu getting together as a couple. The fact that they don't love each other is not a significant piece of this puzzle.

Chris decides the best thing would be for Amanda to leave town quickly. The best thing no doubt, but he's not pleased by the thought. Though until this morning they hadn't seen each other in twenty years and he's about to marry another woman, he says under his breath, "At least I'll get to see her this afternoon."

"What was that?" Bob asks, standing, picking up his big hat, and putting it on. He looks like a mixture of Tom Mix and a brown-skinned Pillsbury doughboy wearing a felt oversized Stetson rather than a chef's tall toque.

Chris thinks fast. "I was just saying I wish the wedding were this afternoon."

"Lulu said the same thing this morning. She understands what's at stake here, as do you."

"We'll be great together, I'm sure." Chris closes the blinds and moves to meet Bob at the door that leads to the stairs and foyer below.

"One last thing before you go." Bob pats the overly large sheriff's badge pinned to the deerskin vest stretched across his overly large middle section.

"About my uncle William?"

"Exactly."

William was Chris's father's older brother, Gabriel's eldest son. He converted, allowed himself to become human, in order to marry a human girl many years ago. It is not a difficult thing to do once the decision is made. A federation member only has to offer his or her hand to the human, and if the human takes that hand in his or hers, the federation member becomes human. There is no going back. The change is permanent. Once William left the federation, he had stayed gone and was never seen again.

Chris had known these things even as a child, which was why he withdrew his hand from Amanda that night on the porch when she so clearly needed his support. Even then he had known how much he hurt her, and he still feels badly about it, though he knows it was unavoidable.

Chris answers Bob's question: "I never knew my Uncle William. He had already converted and left the federation before I was born. With my parents gone, Gabriel and the two boys became my only family. My loyalty is to them and, of course, to the portal, which the Rainwater men, of whom I am the last, have been entrusted to watch over."

Bob extends his hand, Chris takes it, and the two men shake. "That's good enough for me, Chris. With you being who you are and Lulu who she is, you two will be the perfect match. Lineage-wise."

Chapter 12

He Dies as All Earthly Creatures Must

Corner Cupboard Café, Friday

Still sitting with Amanda at the table in the window, Jack says that her going to tonight's rehearsal dinner is a good idea. It will give Amanda a chance to make his mother focus on the need to change her vote. After that, everyone could move on with their lives, and he could concentrate on his.

"Do you know why your mother is so against the condemnation? She would be getting top dollar from the town," Amanda asks.

"She's protecting the island for some reason," Jack replies.

"I got the same feeling from talking to her this morning. She spoke to me in a general way. But it sounded like there was something more than just a sentimental attachment going on, something personal."

"I agree. It may be because in the years after we lost my father, we did picnic on the island frequently. Gabriel encouraged us to come over whenever we wished. Some days he would sit with us on his lawn, and we would all remember my dad. He seemed to know my father very well, and his stories about the relationship between my dad, Bill, and his son, John, the fun times they had, helped me get through a bad part of my life. I know my mother admires him, and I must admit, I have an unexplained feeling for that sweet-spirited old man myself, even for that mysterious island of his. Right now, though, there are other more important issues to consider."

"Such as?"

"Why is Bigfoot here and living among us? And is our town safe with him around?"

Intense is an understatement, Amanda thinks, holding up her coffee cup as Ruthie pours. "Okay, then," she says and sips her refill.

Across the street on the town square lawn, Chris joins Cleo and her tourists near the Bigfoot sculpture. Cleo introduces the Bigfoot-costumed Chris to her people and explains that the man who wins the canoe race around Rainwater Island at the festival each year gets to portray Bigfoot at the next year's festival, as Dr. Rainwater is doing today. This is Chris's eighth year in a row as the town's Bigfoot for the festival. Only Gabriel Rainwater, Chris's grandfather, has won more times. No one really knows how many but in the double digits for sure.

"More like *has to* portray rather than gets to," Chris says, to the group's amusement.

The mother of the little tourist girl raises her hand. "Mr. Bigfoot, my daughter wonders, are you good or bad?"

Chris looks at Cleo. "You want to take that one?"

"Native American lore tells us Bigfoot is here to help and to guide us and, when needs be, to protect us," Cleo replies.

The skunk from the canoe has crossed the street and starts down Coal Creek Alley behind the Corner Cupboard. Ruthie comes out the back door with an armful of trash, not watching where she is going. She steps on a banana peel and starts to slip. The skunk shapeshifts into Gabriel in his human form. He reaches the very pregnant Ruthie, before she hits the ground, and saves her from a nasty fall.

"Be careful there, girl. That's precious cargo you're carrying there."

"Thank you, Dr. Rainwater. You're pretty fast on your feet …"

"For an old guy like me?"

"Old or young, one thing I do know is there aren't many guys like you."

"I'd have to agree with you there, Ruthie."

Ruthie gives the out-of-breath Gabriel a grateful hug.

On the square, the tourist mother says to Cleo, "You mean like the forest rangers watch out for the animals in the woods?"

Cleo continues her explanation: "Yes, very like that and even more."

"So, what's the answer?" Chris asks the tour participants.

"Good," they answer as a group.

"Good," the shy little tourist girl confirms.

Francis has been watching Amanda and Jack through the front window of the café. He noses in through the front screen door to see what's up. The three Firth boys, ages three, five, and seven, immediately spot the big dog and pounce, grabbing his ears and stubby tail. He licks their smiling little Firth faces until they retreat.

"Why are some people in such a rush to get married?" Amanda finally asks Jack as she looks through the window at the fully costumed Chris.

"My thoughts entirely," Jack replies, talking about Lulu. "It's not like Chris and Lulu haven't known each other their whole lives, and now, all the sudden, they decide last week they have to get married this weekend."

"What's that all about?" Amanda asks.

"That's what I've been wondering," Jack replies.

Francis crawls under a nearby table and listens to their conversation. Suddenly the oldest Firth boy again grabs Francis's tail and gets pulled around the floor of the café, with the younger two brothers in pursuit. Francis is there to eavesdrop, not to play grab-my-backsides with a pack of unruly Firths, so he shakes off the gang of rowdy little boys and returns to his place of concealment.

Across the street on the square, it's the tourist father's turn to question Chris and Cleo. "Does Bigfoot ever die?"

Chris answers first. "He does live a long time, that's true. Eventually, however, he dies, as all earthly creatures must."

"Then why hasn't anyone ever found his bones?"

"My husband reads a lot," the tourist mother says.

"The answer is much simpler than you'd think. When the need arises, Bigfoot has the power to become something other than what you see at that moment."

Inside the hardware store, Sam Summertime strains to put a box of light bulbs on a high shelf. Chip is sitting on the box, holding one of the bulbs. Clara watches her husband with anxious eyes as the box begins to tilt and Chip to slide off. She immediately changes into her much taller Bigfoot form, reaches up, saves the box, and catches the bulb and Chip. She tucks Chip into her husband's front shirt pocket and hands the bulb to Sam. Then she changes back into her human form.

"Be more careful, won't you, my dears?"

"Yes, sweet. And thank you," Sam replies.

Chip smiles. He's trying to do better, but so far it isn't working.

Back on the square, the tourist father wonders about Bigfoot's ability to change forms.

"Why have I never heard about that?"

"I can't tell you that," Chris says.

"Why is that?"

"Because you don't have permission to know."

"From whom?"

"I can't tell you that either."

"I don't understand," the tourist father says.

"It's complicated," Cleo interjects.

The tourist father clears his throat, suggesting doubt. "Okay, then. So, when a Bigfoot dies—"

"At the ripe old age of a hundred and seventy-five or so, he might choose to become a bear or an elk," Chris says and holds out his arm. Shoo dives from the sky and lands there. "Or a bird."

"Or even a ma—" Cleo starts.

But Chris interrupts. "Whoa there, girl, let's not give away all my secrets."

Chapter 13

I Like this Town, Mother

Corner Cupboard Café, Friday

Sitting at their table in the window, Jack and Amanda watch Chris across the street. Jack raises his camera and takes a picture through the glass of the young doctor in full Bigfoot costume.

"Chris seems to enjoy being Bigfoot," Amanda says.

"You might say he's a natural," Jack agrees. "The night your mother died, remember what happened to you out on the lake?"

"I remember my canoe being swamped and me falling out. When I was underwater, I remember a large figure swimming toward me." She continues, "I know it was Chris who eventually pulled me out of the water, but who I saw beneath the surface I've never really known."

"It was Bigfoot. I saw him dive in."

"You really think Bigfoot is real?"

"I know he is, and what's more, I know where he lives. And I'm pretty sure I know who he is."

"What do you mean by 'who he is'?"

"I mean Bigfoot has the power to change from his human

form into his beastly form and back again whenever he wishes. I've seen him do it."

"You're saying that ...?"

"When Rainwater Island goes under water, I'll find out for sure if I'm right."

Amanda realizes that Jack is implying that somebody on Rainwater Island is Bigfoot. Gabriel, not very likely. Perhaps more likely, Chris himself. And, as nutty as that sounds, she knows it's not a good time to tell Cleo's son he's gone off the rails. The best thing to do is to play along with Jack's musings until she can get Cleo to change her vote.

"You really believe what you just said?"

"I do, and I'd stake Bigfoot's life on it. I'm a very good shot with my bow."

Francis is getting an unpleasant earful as the cat jumps into Amanda's lap, her collar bell tinkling.

"So, what's Ebay's special talent?" Amanda asks.

"She's a Bigfoot sniffer!"

Jack's last comment is too much for Francis. He needs to end this conversation, so he grabs Amanda's purse in his mouth and runs for the door.

"Hey, Frank, come back with my purse!" Amanda shouts and starts after the big dog. Ruthie picks up Amanda's uneaten blueberry muffin and joins the chase, with her three young sons in pursuit.

Francis and Amanda exit the front screen door first, followed by Ruthie and her three boys, who nearly knock down the family from Cleo's walking tour. Francis drops Amanda's purse and lopes off.

Ruthie talks to Amanda as she leans down to recover her purse: "You forgot your muffin, sweetie."

Shoo swoops down from the sky, spears the muffin with his beak, and lumbers away to the amazement of Ruthie's three sons and the little tourist girl.

The little tourist girl tugs her mother's sleeve and says in a firm voice, "I like this town, Mother."

"It is fun, isn't it, sweetheart?"

Chapter 14

Love Always Matters

Rainwater Medical Clinic, Friday

A block up Elk from the Cupboard is Gabriel's old office, now occupied by Chris and his nurse, Lulu Big Sky. The sign in front of the colorful split log building with a blue door and blue window trim reads, *Medical Clinic, Chris Rainwater, MD, General Practice* and below that, *Lulu Big Sky, RN, Nurse Practitioner, Midwife.*

Francis arrives and noses his way through the front door. A short time later, Chris, still in his costume, crosses the street and follows Francis inside. With the headpiece under his arm, he finds Francis lying on a cowhide-covered couch. The clinic's waiting room is typical of western Colorado physicians' office décor—sturdy furniture crafted by local carpenters and colorful photographs, taken by local photographers, of horses running, waterfalls falling, and an old rust-covered pickup truck sitting beside a wooden-rail fence surrounded by a potpourri of springtime wildflowers.

Francis looks at Chris and shakes his big head.

"Okay, Francis, you're right. We need to talk," Chris says and puts down the costume headpiece.

Francis changes into his easily recognizable Bigfoot form,

furry and black with a thick English neck. He looks a lot like the photograph of a black bear hanging on the wall behind him. "Call me Frank from now on."

"I regret that already," Chris replies, as the odd twosome heads for the back room.

"Frank sounds manlier than Francis," Bigfoot Francis says.

"You're a dog," Chris replies.

"Amanda is back in town."

"I know that. What of it?"

"You're still nuts about each other. That's what of it."

"You're the one that's nuts."

"That may well be, but I saw your faces when you two bumped into each other on the street this morning."

"We? You did that on purpose didn't you?"

"Just trying to help. Even a dog can see you two still love each other."

Chris hesitates. How can that be true? They were just kids when they last saw each other. But he must admit the good feelings are still there, despite the passage of the years. Yet, he knows he must marry Lulu tomorrow evening, whether he and Amanda love each other or not. Love isn't what matters here.

Chris enters the back room. "Love doesn't matter now."

Bigfoot Francis follows him in. "Love always matters."

"You're starting to sound like Gabriel."

"I'll take that as a compliment."

"You need to mind your own business."

"What happens to my best friend is my business."

Bigfoot Francis and Chris take seats at a small table by the window that opens onto the alley. There is an unfinished game on the checkerboard in front of them. Bigfoot Francis is playing the black. Most of his pieces are on the board and have crowns. Chris is red. He has five remaining checkers, none of which is crowned.

"Let's finish the game," Bigfoot Francis says and makes the first move. He takes a single red checker. Chris is now down to four. "Your turn."

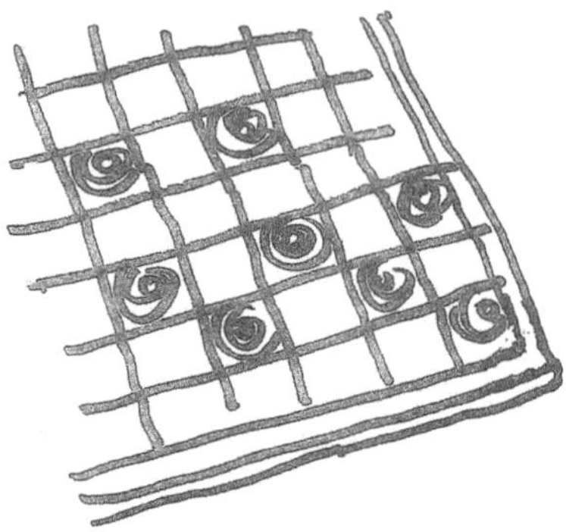

In the alley, Shoo, severely overloaded with Ruthie's muffin, flies toward the doctor's office. He's aiming for the open back room window and flaps his wings to gain enough altitude to clear his stolen pastry over the high ledge. As he ascends, he passes the skunk from Chris's canoe climbing a stack of empty cardboard boxes, heading for the same window. For a second, jaybird and skunk see eye to eye. Then Shoo rises and leaves the gravity-bound stink merchant behind.

Inside the back room, Chris studies the board as Shoo flies through the window with his purloined muffin. He lands on the tabletop and disrupts the game board. Bigfoot Francis straightens the pieces and eyes the black bird.

"Look out, Shoo. You're messing up the board!"

Shoo changes into his unique Bigfoot form—a long thin neck, skinny legs, a big nose, and thin lips.

He takes a seat at the table. "Sorry, you guys." Bigfoot Shoo says and takes a big Bigfoot bite out of the muffin. "Where does Ruthie manage to find blueberries this time of year?"

The skunk peeks his black-and-white V-marked head in the window as Bigfoot Francis says to Chris, "Take your jump."

"Take your jump," Bigfoot Shoo echoes.

"I'm thinking about it."

"Think about this, then. You're about to marry the wrong girl," Bigfoot Francis says.

"Marry the wrong girl," Bigfoot Shoo reiterates. His next

favorite thing to do, after eating blueberry muffins, is to repeat what has just been said.

Chris jumps a single black piece and puts it in his small pile. Bigfoot Francis jumps Chris's four remaining red pieces and clears the board. Game over.

"I win," Bigfoot Francis says.

"He wins," Bigfoot Shoo confirms as if he were a Shadow Mountain Valley echo.

"He always wins," Chris says. He goes to the coffee pot, with his back to the two Bigfoot boys.

Bigfoot Shoo gets Bigfoot Francis's attention and points to the box-climbing skunk listening in at the window. They shapeshift into dog and jaybird.

Chris pours himself a cup of coffee. "Grandfather is sick, boys, much sicker than he lets on. As next in line, when the time comes, it's going to be up to me to take his place. My marrying Lulu would go a long way toward uniting the federation in our struggle to protect our portal. I can't afford to think about my personal feelings right now, whatever they may or may not be."

Not listening, the dog and bird rush out the window after the fleeing skunk.

Chris turns to find the room empty. "Boys? Where'd you go?"

Chapter 15

We Didn't Realize It Was You

Coal Creek Alley, Friday

Francis races after the retreating skunk on the ground, while Shoo tracks him from the air. Francis closes in, knocking over trash cans and chasing the skunk up and down outside staircases. The skunk finally comes to Coal Creek and crosses it boldly by climbing a slender-trunked aspen, bending it down, and launching himself across the stream.

Francis tries to jump the creek and ends up in the water and must swim out. Meanwhile, the skunk slips into an old unused carriage house. Shoo spots him and leads Francis to the skunk's hideout.

Shoo and Francis shapeshift into their Bigfoot forms and block the skunk's exit.

"Gotcha," Bigfoot Francis says to the skunk.

The skunk changes into Gabriel's human form.

Bigfoot Shoo deflates. "Uh-oh."

"Gabriel. We didn't realize it was you," Bigfoot Francis says.

"That was the point," Gabriel replies.

"Chris is marrying Lulu because he thinks he has to."

"I know," Gabriel replies.

"He knows," Bigfoot Shoo says, doing it again.

"Cut that out, Shoo," Bigfoot Francis says.

"Cut what out?" Bigfoot Shoo replies.

"That."

"What?"

"Never mind."

Chapter 16

This Ain't Over Yet

Good Bear Lake Volunteer Firehouse, Friday

Just inside the open, high double doors, Rev. Dinky Round Rock is decorating the town's only fire truck for tomorrow's Bigfoot Days parade. Dinky is a humble man, but there are two things in which he takes pride: his fireworks display on the last day of the festival and this truck, which he drives every year in the Saturday morning parade. The old truck, like most of the town's public equipment, just squeaks by, a holdover from the '70s. It has a reworked motor and gets a set of new hoses, a fresh battery, and four new tires every few years. Yet, the old vehicle has never let the volunteer fire crew down and is Rev. Round Rock's pet project. Every year he looks forward to shining it up, slapping on streamers, and showing it off to the visitors at the Bigfoot Festival parade. Dinky has been at it since the crack of dawn, and he's in no mood for Jack's bizarre anti-Bigfoot behavior today. Plus, Lulu is waiting for Jack in his office, and Dinky suspects that meeting is not going to go well.

Jack enters the firehouse, carrying his bow and quiver. He stops and looks across the open space, toward the stuffed bear standing in the far corner. The bear has an umpire's chest protector hanging around its neck with a big red heart painted on the front. This is Jack's favorite Bigfoot-sized target for practice. Nocking an arrow onto the bow string, he aims and fires. The arrow arcs above Dinky and his truck and strikes the center of the stuffed bear's red heart. The shot is an accurate one but too close for Dinky's comfort.

"Cut that out, Jack," he says.

"Don't worry, Dink. I never miss at this range," Jack replies.

"There's always a first time. And I don't want any new holes in me or my truck." Dinky moves out of the flight path.

"Sure, Dink. Sorry."

"Say," Dinky says. "Does this cat belong to you? She's getting fur all over my newly vacuumed cab." He points at Ebay, who is sprawled over the front seat of the spanking-clean vehicle.

"Yeah, and she's been a big waste of money so far." Jack reaches inside the truck, lifts Ebay out, and tucks her under his arm.

"Thanks," Dinky says as Jack walks away. "Oh, and Lulu's waiting for you in your office."

"It's about time. Maybe she can make some sense out of all this."

"I wouldn't count on it," Dinky says, mostly to himself.

Carrying Ebay, Jack takes big steps down the inside hall until he comes to the office with his name on the glass upper half of the door: *Jack Newday, Fire Captain.* He enters the small space, which is filled with stuffed animal heads and looks more like a taxidermist's shop than the office of a volunteer fire captain. Ebay looks at Jack's animal trophies, hops down, crawls under the desk, and covers her head with her paws.

Waiting for Jack inside is Lulu Big Sky. As Becky Proudlow has suggested, Lulu is a pretty girl with long black hair and big brown eyes. She has bronze skin the color of her father's, although the Native American coloring is a good deal more attractive on Lulu than it is on Pillsbury Bob in his Tom Mix hat.

Jack and Lulu have liked each other since they were kids. Lulu is looking at the three framed photos on Jack's desk: one of the two of them as children, paddling a canoe; another of them as teenagers, dancing at the school prom; and the last of them as adults, kissing under the Christmas mistletoe.

Jack puts away his bow and quiver.

Lulu picks up the photo of them kissing. "I just came by to pick this up and to tell you why I'm marrying Chris."

Ebay eases out from under the desk, apparently curious to hear the explanation.

"Can't wait to hear," Jack replies, knowing there is no reason that would lessen the hurt. He and Lulu are meant for each other, and he has always thought they both knew it. Until last week when her wedding to Chris was announced, Jack would have bet his red pickup against a half-eaten package of Twinkies that the next wedding in town was going to be theirs.

"Because it's important to my father that I do."

Ouch. Ebay crawls back under the desk and tucks her head back under her paws.

Jack grabs the frame of the kissing photo Lulu is holding. "And why would that be?"

"It's complicated."

"Try me."

"I can't. Now give me my picture." She pulls at the photograph.

"No. It's my picture too."

Dinky was right. Lulu's reason makes no sense at all. Sure, she is an old-fashioned girl, and she values her family—two of the things Jack likes the most about her. But she is also a grown girl and, at least Jack had always thought, his girl. And now she plans to marry Chris because her father wants her to? What is that about? More than just odd, this strange turn of events is ridiculous.

"But, Lulu, your father isn't marrying Bigfoot! You are!" Jack holds onto the picture.

"Jack, that's just silly. You're talking about something you thought you saw in the middle of the night twenty years ago when you were just a boy." She tugs back.

"Dark or not and boy or not, I know what I saw." He tries again to take the kissing photo from her, but Lulu hangs on.

"I'm sorry, Jack, I really am, but there's nothing I can do."

They continue to struggle until Jack finally softens his grip and lets go. "Fine, you take it, then."

"Thanks." She moves to the door. "I should go now."

"Then go," he says even though it's the last thing he wants her to do. But there's no way to argue with the idea that her marriage to Chris is happening just because her father wants it.

"Okay, fine."

"Okay, fine."

Picture in hand, Lulu quietly leaves. Jack waits for a moment and then goes over to his desk, opens the deep lower drawer, and removes an identically framed photo. Ebay comes out and hops onto the desktop as Jack kisses the photo and then sets it beside the other two.

"Did any of that make sense to you?" he asks Ebay, who looks at him with a blank-faced catty stare. "I just don't get it." He picks up his bow and quiver. "One thing I do know, though, cat. This ain't over yet."

Chapter 17

Least Important Person Is Always the Groom

Blue Moon Inn, Friday

Carrying a toolkit and dressed in a flannel shirt and blue jeans, Chris, with Francis at his heels, climbs the front porch steps and stops at the front door of the inn. He remembers his grandfather carving the unusual door with aspens with open eyes and limbs filled with leaves. When Amanda left and locked the door, the aspens closed their eyes and lost their leaves. The door is unlocked again, since Amanda has returned and opened it with her mother's old key, but the aspens' eyes so far remain closed, and the limbs, leafless.

Neither Chris nor Francis has been inside the inn in years. As they enter, they are not surprised to find the old place showing its age and a serious lack of care. Nevertheless, it remains one of the finest and best-built log structures in the town. Chris has always admired the place for its craftsmanship, especially for its woodwork, most of which was done by his grandfather. He particularly likes the Gabriel-carved mantle above the open-faced stone fireplace in the great room. But time has created a lot of work to do in the aging lodge.

Chris and Francis shapeshift into their more productive Bigfoot forms.

"Dust is a foot thick in here," Bigfoot Francis says. "If the roof leaked, you could grow San Luis Valley potatoes on the floors."

"Let's get the downstairs done before Amanda arrives," Bigfoot Chris replies.

In a whirlwind of Bigfoot action, they sweep and mop the floors, replace the broken cords and clean the hand-blown, double-hung windows, rehang the downed window coverings, fix the broken chair legs, upright the dining room table, and reattach the oven door to the wood burning kitchen stove. They use their hairy forearms to remove years of dust from the kitchen's stone countertops. Bigfoot Francis is considerably hairier than Bigfoot Chris and is particularly good at the forearm-assisted dusting chore.

When they finish downstairs, they go up to the front bedroom, where they are greeted by the bed mattress resting on the floor. Bigfoot Chris lifts a corner of the mattress and looks underneath. "I was right." The side boards are warped, and the slats are on the floor. "Where's my toolkit?"

"You left it downstairs," Bigfoot Francis says.

"You mind getting it while I move the mattress?"

"I will if you promise to say something nice to Amanda when you see her."

"Like what?"

Bigfoot Francis starts for the stairs. "Like how much you've missed her."

"I'll think about it."

Bigfoot Chris lifts the mattress to one side. When Bigfoot Francis returns, he fixes the problem with several eyebolts and a spool of heavy wire from his Summertime Hardware's toolbox. As Chris is finishing, he hears Amanda's car pull up in front. Chris and Francis change into their human and dog forms and crawl under the bed to complete the repair.

Amanda enters through the front door. To her surprise, the curtains are up, the floors are mopped, and the windows are clean and working. The dining room table is upright, and the chair legs are fixed. In the kitchen, the counters are dustless, and the oven door has been returned to its hinges. She smiles and heads for the stairs.

Moments later, in the upstairs front bedroom, she finds the bed upright and the mattress in place. She moves to the clothes wardrobe, where she knows her DWA jacket is hanging, and pushes the old door closed until the latch clicks.

In his human form, Chis sticks his head out from under the bed. "I was going to fix that wardrobe door next," he says to Amanda.

He slides out and gets to his feet feeling remarkably good. But what's the point, with his wedding to Lulu coming up in a less than a day? He thinks about saying something nice to Amanda, as Francis has lobbied for, but then he decides to say instead, "You know I've really missed…" He hesitates.

Francis sticks his dog's head out from under the bed. He looks hopeful with big eyes.

"Missed what?" Amanda says.

"The inn."

Chris's "missed the inn" comment is an obvious nonstarter for Francis. He frowns.

"I'd forgotten how great this old place is," Chris continues. This is as nice as he feels he can be, with his wedding rehearsal a little more than an hour away.

Francis shakes his big head. Not even close to nice. A total zero, like Chris's lack-luster approach to the problem.

"Frank," Amanda says, petting Francis. "You're here too. Thanks."

"He did help some, but it was mostly me," Chris says.

Francis lies flat on the floor, rolls onto his back, and sticks out his long tongue, making it clear to Chris that he is not only a great big chicken but also a big fat liar.

"It was light today at the office, so I decided I'd come by early and see what I could do."

"It doesn't look like the same place. What was wrong with the bed?"

"Your slats were out."

Francis looks up at Chris as if to say, *Forget the stupid slats and say something meaningful to the girl before it's too late.*

"You were right then."

"Uh-huh."

Hardly meaningful. Francis is losing patience, and he barks, underlining his who-cares-about-the-slats point of view.

"It's these old beds," Chris says. "The side boards have been bent by use through the years and the supporting mattress slats no longer fit. The least bit of weight on the bed causes them to drop through and the mattress falls."

"How do you fix something like that?"

"Easy enough. You just screw eyebolts into the side boards and pull them together with heavy wire until they come straight."

Francis rolls onto his stomach. Chris is about to marry someone he doesn't love and he's giving Amanda a how-to lecture on repairing warped side boards with eyebolts and wire from Sam and Clara's store. *Geesh.*

"Does it work?" Amanda asks.

Chris pats the mattress. "Let's give it a try."

Chris plops down on the bed. Amanda sits beside him. Nothing happens.

"It worked." Amanda observes, as her hand almost touches Chris's.

Francis hops on the bed and wedges between the two, looking at Chris and then at Amanda as if to say, *You two are a waste of time, romance-wise. I'd bite you both if I thought it would help.*

"Almost always does." Chris moves his hand aside.

"How long have you and Lulu been engaged?"

"A week."

"A week?"

"I know it's a short time, but we really didn't have much choice in the matter."

"I don't think I quite understand."

"Let's just say it's complicated." It's the familiar non-answer where Bigfoot questions are concerned, but's it's all Chris can come up with sitting this close to a grown-up Amanda.

"Sounds like it. But thanks again for your trouble." Amanda pets Francis. "You too, Frank."

Francis manages a forced smile, acknowledging her approval and obviously happy with the new name, Frank.

"No trouble at all," Chris says.

Francis jumps off the bed. These two are beyond his abilities as a matchmaker. They are so broken that even Clara Summertime would have tough time fixing them. He crawls out of the room on his all fours.

Amanda stands and looks at her watch. "It's almost five now, and the dinner at the marina starts at six."

Chris moves to the wardrobe and rattles the door. "Are you sure you don't want me to have a go at this old wardrobe? I have a trick to fix that stubborn door."

Amanda puts her hand on the door, keeping it closed. She knows what is hanging just inside. "No, no. You'd better get going if you're going to paddle home and back again in time for your rehearsal."

"No worries. The least important person there is always the groom."

Chapter 18

Unless Ruthie's Baby Comes

Rainwater Island, Friday

Chris rows home. As he walks up the steps from the dock, followed by Francis, he sees Gabriel at the window of his second-floor bedroom, looking out at the lake. Shoo flies over Chris and Francis, lands on Gabriel's arm, and whispers in his ear. They disappear inside the room.

Chris and Francis enter the house and climb the steps to Gabriel's big bedroom. Inside, they find Gabriel in bed, covers pulled to his chin, eyes closed as if he were sleeping. Shoo sits on the tall bedstead, above the herd of Gabriel-carved elk that decorates its face.

"You warned him I was coming, didn't you?" Chris says to Shoo. "Well, it won't do either of you any good." He moves to the bedside, stethoscope in hand, and strips back Gabriel's covers. "Wake up, you faker."

Fully dressed, Gabriel opens his eyes and smiles. The crew in the barn have been in and out of the house all day fussing at him and taking turns guarding the door so he couldn't get out, he complains. "Have you ever tried getting past a single-minded black bear or a bad-tempered great horned owl in a tight hallway when they don't want you to?"

"They were just trying to do their jobs."

"Like I'm just trying to follow my doctor's orders."

"Since when?" Chris listens to Gabriel's chest. "Sounds like a class five rapids in there."

Gabriel's big heart, filled with 175 years of love for others, 150 of those spent as head ranger, is finally failing him. There's nothing more medically Chris can do to stop it. What he said to the tourists in town is true. All of earth's creatures, be they human, animal, or even a head federation ranger, must one day die, and Gabriel's time is close at hand. Chris would need to limit his grandfather's activity as much as Gabriel would let him.

"I'm fine," Gabriel says.

"You're not fine, and you know it. We'll just have to do without you tonight at the rehearsal. You're staying right here until further notice."

"Unless Ruthie's baby comes."

"Of course." This is the one exception. As head ranger, Gabriel will have to go if the portal opens. "I understand."

Gabriel asks a question he already knows the answer to: "Do you know Amanda James is in town?"

"I do. I just left her at the inn. I stopped by and fixed her mother's old collapsed bed."

"Were her slats out?"

Francis nods. Those silly slats again. Like grandson, like grandfather.

"They were."

"Use eyebolts and wire?"

"I did."

Again, Francis nods. Of course, he used eyebolts and wire. What else would a Rainwater man use to fix funky bed slats? Francis jumps off the bed in a huff. Slats, eyebolts, and wire had gotten Chris nowhere with this girl. And going over them again now with his grandfather is not going to help.

"What's the matter with Francis?" Gabriel asks.

"He isn't happy with what I said to Amanda."

"What did you say?"

"Nothing. That's why he's mad."

"How did it feel to see Amanda? I remember how close you two were as youngsters."

"No big deal, really. After all, it's been twenty years."

How could any of this Amanda business change the fact that he is marrying Lulu Big Sky tomorrow? It can't. Yet, Chris knows he's not telling the truth about how he feels. Gabriel knows it too, as does Francis, who now sits at Gabriel's feet, looking suspicious. The big dog barks.

"Francis doesn't seem to agree with you," Gabriel says and pets the dog's black head. "And I'm afraid I don't either."

"You're entitled to your opinions," Chris replies.

"What do you say, Shoo?" Gabriel asks.

Shoo drops from the bedstead onto Francis's neck, and he and Francis shake their heads in unison at Chris.

"Looks like the vote is three to one against you," Gabriel says to Chris.

Chris points his finger at Gabriel and then at Francis and Shoo. "Listen, you furry rabble-rousers, I intend on marrying Lulu Big Sky tomorrow, so what does it matter how I feel about Amanda James today?"

"Let me ask you that same question. What does it matter?"

"It doesn't. And I know what you're thinking: we'll just have to see then, won't we?"

"Couldn't have said it better."

Shoo flutters his thin lips and utters an original Australian jaybird thought. *"Phooey!"*

Chapter 19

That's All Anybody Ever Says

Newday Marina, Friday

Amanda walks along the leaf-covered, aspen-lined path from the inn to the marina as the sun sets behind Shadow Mountain. In the fading light, she sees Chris's canoe leave the island dock across the lake. He is a good ten-minute paddle away. She'll be glad to see him again but would feel better if it weren't at the rehearsal dinner for his wedding to Lulu Big Sky. And she still isn't exactly sure why.

The purpose of her visit to Good Bear Lake is to get Cleo to change her vote, a switch that would result in Rainwater Island going under water. She and Chris are not on the same team. Though the thought of Chris makes her wish they were. And again, she isn't sure just why. And what is this silliness about Chris and Lulu having no choice about marrying quickly because it was complicated? "It's complicated" is what people say when they aren't willing to explain the real reason for their actions. What could that reason be? Cleo probably knows the answer. But would she tell? Judging by her performance today, the likelihood is she wouldn't. Gus is right, the woman, no matter how sweet, is as slippery as Coal Creek Alley in mid-winter.

Amanda looks at the leaf-barren aspens and remembers what Gabriel used to say about this time of year, that everything is about to be new and anything is possible. Everything is new fits Chris and his wedding plans for tomorrow. But anything is possible doesn't seem to be working for her today, as she approaches the marina.

Inside the marina's kitchen, Cleo enters to find Ruthie and Lyle Firth cooking the dinner for tonight's gathering. "How's it going in here, you two?"

"We're in hog heaven," rail-thin Lyle replies.

"Ixnay on the pig jokes, hon," Ruthie says, patting her enormous tummy. She is due at any second, but, as with her other three children, she prefers to work until her water breaks. Holy moly.

On the other side of the swinging door between the kitchen and the dining room, Jack is setting the table. Cleo comes in from the kitchen.

"Why are you being so stubborn about this water thing, Mother? You'd still have plenty to do in town if you gave up the marina," Jack says.

"I know, Jack. This isn't really about the marina. Hopefully, I'll be able to tell you soon the real reason why my answer is no. I'm obligated to wait on permission though, before I can."

"Permission from whom? What does that even mean?'

"It's complicated."

"Here we go again with the 'it's complicated excuse,'" Jack whispers to himself. "Go ahead. I've got all the time in the world," he says to his mother.

After knocking at the front door, Amanda enters and follows Jack's increasingly high-pitched voice into the dining room. "Hope I'm not intruding," she announces.

"No, no, come in and help Jack with the table," Cleo says. "We'll finish this conversation some other time, son."

Amanda hugs Cleo. "Thanks for inviting me. I hope we can talk in a bit. But first—and I know it's none of my business—I have to say I was surprised to hear Chris and Lulu were getting married so quickly." She hadn't meant to open her business conversation with Cleo on an unrelated note, but when she opened her mouth, out it came.

Jack gets louder with his handling of the dinnerware. "You and me both."

"I was talking to Chris this afternoon. He said they didn't really have a choice. I was wondering why that would be?"

"Yeah. Why would that be?" Jack asks his mother.

"It's complicated," Cleo says again.

"That's what Chris said," Amanda says.

"That's all anybody around here ever says," Jack says.

Lulu comes in from the deck, where she's been working with Dinky on ceremony details. Jack sees her, grabs Amanda, and gives her a big kiss. The performance is not lost on Lulu.

Cleo turns Amanda around by the shoulders and pushes her toward the kitchen. "Let's get you out of the line of fire." They duck through the swinging door.

Lulu picks up a stack of plates and begins to put them out. "I see you and Amanda are getting reacquainted," she says to Jack.

"Uh-huh. We have a lot in common. We're both human."

Lulu selects a butter plate and tosses it at Jack, but he catches it midair. Lulu picks up a cup and tosses it. Jack catches the cup in his other hand. Then she tosses a dinner plate. He drops the butter plate and the cup but as he fumbles, he misses the dinner plate. All three pieces of pottery hit the floor and break.

Lulu moves the shards out of the way with her foot. "You should be more careful with your mother's dishes," she says to Jack and pushes open the door to the kitchen.

Chapter 20

Holy Moly

Newday Marina, Friday

As Lulu bristles through the well-used kitchen door, Ruthie puts her hands on her tummy. "Holy Moly. My water just broke."

Cleo, Amanda, Lulu, and Lyle circle around Ruthie.

"Let's get her to the couch in the front room," Lulu says.

Lead by Lulu, the concerned group moves into the main room. Lyle and Cleo help Ruthie to the couch as she goes into labor. Her expression goes from I'm-a-happy Ruthie to I'm-a-don't- touch-me Ruthie.

Chris comes through the door from the kitchen. "Hello, everybody. Have I missed anything?"

Lulu has her ear on Ruthie's tummy. "Ruthie has started her labor."

Chris knows this means the portal will be opening soon and Gabriel will have to respond. He knows the boys will be there for him. Nonetheless, he fears the exertion might be too much for his sick, aging grandfather and wishes he could help but knows he can't. Only the head ranger can bring a new human spirit into the world.

Lulu directs her comments to Ruthie and Lyle: "Take her

home, put her to bed, but stay close. And, Ruthie, remember to breathe slowly in and out through your mouth."

Lyle starts breathing in and out slowly through his mouth.

"Call me when the contractions are three minutes apart."

The glassy-eyed Lyle is still breathing hard, in and out.

"Better make that five minutes," Lulu adds. "Remember, you two, this is Ruthie's fourth baby and her labor could be brief."

"I'm for that," Ruthie adds.

"No worries. We got this one," Lyle says.

"Who is we?" Ruthie wonders aloud through a grimace.

Chapter 21

Didn't Hurt A Bit

Rainwater Island, Friday

Gabriel struggles out of bed, coughing. He looks outside and sees the big windows on the back of the barn glowing blue. He opens the door to the hall and shouts to Francis and Shoo, "Hey, boys, saddle up! Ruthie's having her baby!"

Gabriel, followed by Francis with Shoo on his back, hastens from the house and across the lawn to the barn. They enter the cavernous space, and the wooden animals awaken. The cougar and elk stand side by side, as do the bear and the bighorn sheep, and so on throughout the tall-ceilinged barn. The three big birds on the high limbs of the fir tree, Red, Honk, and Who, float down and fall in behind the dog, jaybird, and the others. They all follow Gabriel to the doorway to the basement portal.

At a wave of Gabriel's right hand, the animated animals, including Francis and Shoo, remain behind as he starts down the steps. At the bottom of the staircase, he changes into his Bigfoot form. He puts his right hand, the hand with the leather wristband, flat against the door. The door, already partially open, opens widely. Blue light pours out and washes over Bigfoot Gabriel.

The smell of piñon pine follows the light and the low guttural sound of a prowling puppy is heard. Bigfoot Gabriel enters the light and disappears into the portal, the pathway for the coming, as well as the going, of human spirits in and out of this world. Moments later, Bigfoot Gabriel emerges cradling Ruthie's spirit child in his arms. The animals remain quiet and still as Bigfoot Gabriel and the spirit child ascend the stairway. Francis and Shoo shapeshift into their Bigfoot forms, haloed by the ethereal blue light that now fills the barn. They follow Bigfoot Gabriel and the spirit child through the rear door, onto the barn porch, and into the chilly night. Blue light floods through the ancient windows, out the back door, and down the steps toward the lake.

In her room on the second floor of the Corner Cupboard, Ruthie lies quietly in bed. Lyle turns out the lights.

"I'll be just outside, sweet." He turns and walks into the door frame. *Thud.* "I'm good. Didn't hurt a bit." Then he does it again. *Thud.* "That did," he says and picks up an ice bag from the hall table, puts it on his forehead, and lies on the couch in the living room.

Outside the café in Coal Creek Alley, the moon has changed from autumnal orange to portal blue. Bigfoot Gabriel and his entourage step from the cloud of blue that has transported them across the lake.

"You two, wait here and be quiet," Bigfoot Gabriel says to the two shapeshifted Bigfoot boys.

Bigfoot Shoo jars the lid of a trash can, causing a metallic clatter.

"*Shhhhh,*" Bigfoot Gabriel

says as he steps into the illuminated channel of blue headed toward the café.

"*Shhhhh*," Bigfoot Francis says to Bigfoot Shoo.

"*Shhhhh*," Bigfoot Shoo says to himself.

"Quit that," Bigfoot Francis adds.

"Quit what?"

In the dark of Ruthie's bedroom, Bigfoot Gabriel exits the light and places the spirit child into a sleeping Ruthie's waiting tummy. He then leaves the way he came, in a puff of blue, out through the window. Ruthie suddenly awakens as the last wisp of blue retreats from her room.

"Lyle, call Lulu!" she shouts. "It's time!"

At the marina on the shore of the lake, Lulu and Chris come onto the deck where Rev. Dinky waits.

"Sorry to keep you waiting, Dinky," Chris says. "Ruthie's gone into labor, and Lyle has driven her home."

"No problem," Dinky replies. "We've lost our maid of honor," he adds, meaning Ruthie. "But at least our bride and groom are still here."

Cleo, Lulu, and Jack watch Chris and Amanda eye each other as the big yellow moon over the lake fades to blue, reflecting the flood of light coming from the island onto the surface of the water.

Chapter 22

You May Kiss the Bride

Newday Marina, Friday

Lulu's cell phone rings. She listens and, after a moment, punches off. "That was Lyle. I have to go."

"Cleo, what should we do?" Dinky asks.

"How about Jack drives Lulu over to the Cupboard and Chris stays behind to finish up?" Cleo says. "Amanda, would you stand in for the bride?"

The blue moon is in full bloom. Chris and Amanda look at each other. Sounds okay to them. Sounds better than okay. Sounds warm and good.

"No problem," Dinky says.

A tsunami of pure love is flowing in from the island, covering the water and the face of the moon, washing onto the deck of the marina, and rushing along with Jack and Lulu toward the town.

At the door of the Proudlow Real Estate Office, Tom Throttle removes his hat and sticks his head inside. "Hey, Beck, how about you and me grabbing a bite of supper together?"

"Love to, Tom."

He puts out his boney hand, and Becky takes it in her fleshy one.

"What's the blue moon all about?" she asks.

"I don't know, but I love it."

"Love is just the right word."

Jack and Lulu arrive at the Corner Cupboard in Jack's red pickup truck. He offers Lulu his hand to help her down. She refuses to take it and gets out on her own. Covered in blue, a frustrated Jack follows her to the front door of the café, where they are greeted by Lyle holding a bag of ice.

"How is Ruthie doing?" Lulu asks.

"Great. This baby stuff is old hat to us Firths," Lyle answers, replacing the ice bag onto his head.

On the deck at the marina, Rev. Dinky presses on with the rehearsal. Only he, Chris, and Amanda remain. Cleo has gone to the kitchen to clean up.

"Then we exchange vows, *blah, blah, blah*," Dinky says.

"I do," Chris says, looking at Amanda.

"Not yet you don't. Not until just before the 'you may kiss the bride' part."

"What part is that?" Amanda asks.

"You may kiss the bride," Dinky says hesitatingly, but it's already too late to slow the cascade of events that is occurring as the world of Good Bear Lake becomes totally engulfed in blue light.

In the marina kitchen, Cleo stands at the sink, washing dishes. She reaches for the lone photo standing on the counter. It's of her husband, Bill. She picks up his picture, looks out the window at the gigantic blue moon over the lake, and kisses the glass.

"Things are moving right along, Bill. Our boy, Jack, is going to be just fine."

She returns the picture to the counter and dries a dish.

On the deck, Dinky watches as, by the light of blue moon, Chris and Amanda look at each other longingly and in the next moment are lost in a soulful kiss that goes on and on. And on.

In town, in the upstairs bedroom at the Cupboard, Lyle beams at son number four as Jack ushers the other three Firth boys in to see their mother and new baby brother.

"Hey, guys. One more of these little rascals and we got ourselves our own basketball team," Lyle says.

With one eye open and one closed, Ruthie manages to give Lyle a dirty look. "Don't go there, Lyle Firth!"

On the marina deck, Dinky holds his forehead as the blue moon fades. Chris and Amanda end their prolonged kiss and share another prolonged look.

"Now this could be a problem," Dinky says.

Chapter 23

Blame It on the Blue Moon

Ranger Hall, Saturday

Clouds hide the mountaintops that surround the town of Good Bear Lake. There is rain in the forecast for the afternoon, after this morning's fall festival parade. By now, everybody in town knows what happened yesterday, the good and the bad, including Ruthie's new baby being born and Chris and Amanda's big rehearsal dinner snafu.

The question around town, including in the directors meeting room at Ranger Hall, is what about the wedding between Chris and Lulu? Will it take place as scheduled today or not?

Gabriel, Chris, Francis, Lulu, Bob Big Sky, Rev. Dinky Round Rock, and Sam and Clara Summertime take their seats around the circular table. Chip hops down from Sam's pocket but has trouble getting into his chair. Shoo flies in through the door, deposits Chip in his proper place, and sits in his regular seat beside Francis. Everyone places a hand, a paw, or a wing on the tabletop.

As the table begins to glow a faint blue, each takes his or her individual Bigfoot form, each retaining his or her personal idiosyncrasies. The tall stay tall, the small stay small, and so on. Shoo is late and redundant, and Chip, clumsy. Francis knows it all, he thinks. And Bob still gets right to the point. Precise and complete, as always.

"Before we get started, I'd like to salute our head ranger for the job he did for Ruthie and Lyle and their new baby. Great work, Gabriel, as always," Bigfoot Bob says to applause from the room, which is now filled with ten three-fingered Bigfoot ranger directors. "I guess you know why we're here, Chris?" he adds.

"Yes, and I want to say how sorry I am to everybody and especially to you, Lulu, for my outrageous behavior last night. I don't know what came over me," Bigfoot Chris says.

Bigfoot Francis holds up his hand. "I do."

"He does," echoes Bigfoot Shoo.

"Hush," Bigfoot Francis says to Bigfoot Shoo.

"The chair recognizes Francis," Bigfoot Bob says.

"It's Frank," Bigfoot Francis says.

"It's Frank," Bigfoot Shoo reiterates.

"Excuse me?" Bigfoot Bob says.

"Never mind that now," Bigfoot Francis says. "I just want a word here. It was the blue moon."

"That's four words," Bigfoot Shoo says.

"Five, actually," Bigfoot Chip points out.

Bigfoot Shoo counts on his Bigfoot fingers, one, two, three on one hand and two on the other. "Five, actually," he repeats.

Meanwhile, at the shore of the lake, in the kitchen of the Blue Moon Inn, Cleo stands at the wood-burning stove, frying eggs in a pan. She's making a favorite of Amanda's mother for breakfast, fried egg sandwiches.

"Thanks for coming over to feed me," Amanda says from where she sits at the table. "Now can you tell me what happened to us at the rehearsal last night?"

No one is more surprised than Amanda by her actions. She is supposedly here to get Cleo to change her vote, not to become involved in Chris's life.

"Your mother would have blamed what you two did on the blue moon."

"You're saying a natural phenomenon like a blue moon can make two people do something crazy like we did? And on the day before Chris's wedding to Lulu?"

"I'm just saying it's a possibility."

"Not for a girl like me."

"What kind of girl is that?"

Cleo finishes putting together a pair of fried egg sandwiches and hands one to Amanda, who takes a big bite. Chewing, she says, "Thanks. A well thought out one."

"Thought out by whom?" Cleo refills their coffee cups and sits beside Amanda with her own sandwich.

"My father, I guess. He always says to think with your head and not your heart. I suppose I'm a lot like him in that respect."

Amanda's mother was a hopeful romantic, but her father is just the opposite, which had a lot to do with their divorce. That and her father's driving ambition to succeed on the larger Denver stage. Amanda has always thought that she takes after her father. Though it's starting to look like just the opposite may be true.

"Judging by your performance last night, you might want to rethink that assessment of yourself," Cleo observes.

At Ranger Hall, the meeting of the Bigfoot directors continues. Bigfoot Chris is uncertain, while Bigfoot Francis appears confident. Bigfoot Shoo again counts on his fingers and whispers, "Five for sure," to Bigfoot Francis.

"Five. We got it, Shoo," Bigfoot Francis replies.

"That's my defense? It was the blue moon?" Bigfoot Chris glares at Bigfoot Francis.

"Give it a chance."

"A blue moon is the result of pure love being released into the world. We all know that," Bigfoot Lulu says. "It's the most powerful force there is on this earth."

"No argument there," Bigfoot Clara says.

"I can certainly understand how something like this might have happened, given that influence," Bigfoot Lulu adds.

"See there," Bigfoot Francis says to Bigfoot Chris.

"See there," Bigfoot Shoo says to himself.

"This marriage will do nothing but strengthen the federation at this critical time for the portal, and I'm content to have it go forward," Bigfoot Lulu adds.

All in the room applaud. *Clap, clap.*

"Hear, hear," Bigfoot Dinky says.

"Hear, hear," Bigfoot Sam agrees.

"Hear, hear," Bigfoot Shoo piles on.

As the meeting concludes, the directors return to their usual forms and exit through the door. Last out are Lulu and Gabriel. They come down the portrait-lined staircase together. Lulu has a question for him.

"I've always heard that if a federation member wants to convert, to become human, all they have to do is offer their hand to a human, and if the human takes their hand, then the federation member becomes human. Is that true?"

"Yes."

"I've also heard that it works both ways. A human, if they really desire it, can become federation by offering their hand to one of us. And if we chose to accept it, then the human becomes federation."

"That is true too. But remember, in either case, the change is permanent. Once the choice has been made, there's no going back."

At the kitchen table at the inn, Cleo finishes her coffee and jumps up. "Got to run. It's parade day."

"Oh," Amanda says, "I was hoping we'd have a chance to talk this morning about your vote last week at the council meeting. I was thinking that you and I might—"

"I'd be happy to chat with you later today, sweet, but right now I have to decorate lamp posts. I really should have done that last night, but then things got nutty."

Cleo bolts out the back door, letting the screen door slam behind her. In a flash, she is in the woods and gone.

"She did it again," Amanda says as she puts her dishes in the sink. She starts for the stairs to get ready for the parade.

Upstairs in her bedroom, Amanda stands for a moment at the window, looking across the lake at the island. Then she shakes her head, opens the wardrobe, and removes her DWA jacket.

"It's time for me to let people know who I work for and why I'm here." She puts the jacket on, looks in the mirror on the back of the wardrobe door, touches the DWA logo above the pocket, and adds, "That includes you, Chris Rainwater."

Chapter 24

Unless You Really Are Bigfoot

Elk Avenue, Saturday.

The fall festival parade is in full swing. Crowds line both sides of Elk Avenue as the participants move slowly by. Once again wearing his full Bigfoot costume, Chris leads off in a hay wagon he shares with a local country band, the Bigfoot Boys. The wagon is being pulled by a tractor driven by Sam Summertime. Chip rides with Sam, again ensconced in Sam's shirt pocket.

When the tractor hits a pothole in the street, Chip bounces out and lands on a hay bale on top of the wagon. Chris sees him fly out and fall. He picks him up.

"You okay, Chip?" he says to the fuzzy little fellow.

Chip smiles and nods an I'm fine. Chris hands him to Sam, who tucks him back into his high pocket loft and drives on. Once again, no harm, no foul for Chipmunk Who Falls A Lot.

Next in line is Dinky behind the wheel of his hand-decorated, old-time fire truck. Sheriff Bob Big Sky and his daughter, Lulu, ride on the running boards, waving at the crowd and tossing candy to the kids, several of whom are dressed in costume, some as animals and some as other things like princesses, superheroes, and such. Ruthie has the two oldest Firth boys decked out in home-made miniature Bigfoot gear. In standard Bigfoot fashion, they chase the local girls in and out between the parade vehicles. The little tourist girl leaves her parents on the sidewalk and joins in the chase, squealing just as loudly as the other Bigfoot-pursued young females.

"Be careful, sweetheart!" the tourist mother shouts with no obvious effect.

The fire truck is followed by Tom Throttle at the reins of a horse-drawn stagecoach. Becky sits up top in the driver's seat beside Tom. The Good Bear Lake Chamber of Commerce logo is emblazoned on the passenger doors on both sides. Gus Cobb rides inside the coach, waving at the crowd. He's wearing a baseball cap with the DWA logo above the bill. Shoo swoops in through the coach window, snatches the cap, and flies out the opposite side, leaving the baldheaded Gus bareheaded.

In the crowd, weaving in and out of a mass of legs, Francis manages to stay just ahead of Jack's cat, Ebay, her little collar bell tinkling. Ebay appears to be stalking Francis. Francis has decided it's because she's a Bigfoot sniffer like Jack said yesterday at the café. Not wanting to take any chances, he picks up the pace. Ebay stays on his trail.

Francis turns up Coal Creek Alley behind the doctor's office and shapeshifts into his Bigfoot form. As Ebay turns the corner, Bigfoot Francis jumps from behind a pile of empty cardboard boxes and shouts, "*Boo!*" Ebay's eyes get big. She turns tail, literally, and races back to Elk Avenue, raising dust with her flashing paws as she runs.

"That should do it," Bigfoot Francis says. He changes back into a dog and follows the scrambling cat into the crowd, where Ebay has joined the gaggle of girls being chased by the two junior Bigfoot-costumed Firth boys.

In the food tent on the city hall lawn, Lyle Firth stokes the smoldering coals in his fat half-barrel black metal barbecue pit. This morning he's smoking turkeys, his wife's favorite. He pulls off a drumstick, takes a big bite, and waves at Ruthie with the rest.

Ruthie is sitting on the upstairs porch of the Corner Cupboard across the street, feeding their new son. Ruthie returns Lyle's wave and says to her new baby, "When you grow up, dear, promise me never to wave at your wife with her lunch's leg, okay?"

At the four-way stop at the beginning of Elk Avenue, Jack holds a ladder for Cleo, who is decorating a lamp post, even though the parade has moved on.

"The parade is long gone, Mom," Jack says, pointing up the street.

"I know, son, but a Newday never does anything halfway. Toss me up that red roll."

Jack tosses her the blue one. "I hear Lulu and Chris's wedding is still on."

"And why shouldn't it be? I said the red roll."

They trade. She swirls red crepe paper around the lamp post.

"Because the groom isn't who he seems to be is why."

"People often aren't, Jack. Now the blue."

Frustrated, Jack tosses her up the blue. "Yeah, but Chris isn't people."

The parade has ended, and the crowd has congregated in the town square. Chris, dressed as Bigfoot in full costume, stands with Gus and Tom on the hay wagon. They listen as the Bigfoot Boys finish their final song, Blue Moon of Good Bear Lake, sung to the tune of Blue Moon of Kentucky. Chris can see Amanda coming toward the wagon as the Bigfoot Boys sing: "*It is on a moonlight night, the stars are shining bright, they whispered from on high, your love has said goodbye.*"

Amanda approaches, and Chris removes his headpiece to

watch as she works her way through the crowd. The Bigfoot Boys conclude their song with: "*Blue moon of Good Bear Lake, keep on shining, shine on the one that's gone and left me blue.*"

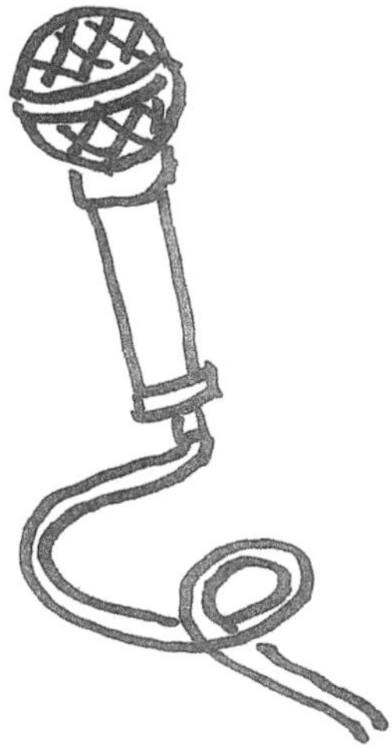

Tom disconnects the microphone from its stand. "Let's hear it for Good Bear Lake's own Bigfoot Boys."

The crowd applauds and cheers.

Tom continues, "Each year the chamber sponsors an annual Bigfoot Days debate at this time. Today's topic is the Denver Water Authority's plan for our lake. Is it good or bad for our community? Speaking for the affirmative will be Gus Cobb, the DWA regional director. And against, Dr. Chris Rainwater, our own Bigfoot Days Bigfoot."

Tom hands Gus the mic as Shoo lands on Chris's arm. Chris recovers Gus's hat.

Gus says into the mic, "There's someone here much better suited than I to make this argument. She's in town to help us get this deal done. How about it, folks? Help me bring her up?"

Amanda, now wearing her DWA jacket, makes her way up the steps and onto the wagon. Chris looks at the DWA logo on Gus's cap and then at the logo over the pocket of Amanda's jacket. He makes the connection and hands the cap to Gus.

"Thanks," Gus says and covers his baldpate. He introduces Amanda to the crowd: "Please welcome Amanda James, the little girl from Good Bear Lake who has made it big in Denver at the DWA."

The crowd responds with applause. And a few boos.

Chris now realizes that Amanda is the water authority's "best man," the person Gabriel warned him would be coming to town. She is obviously here to get Cleo to change her vote. She is the enemy, yet it still feels good just to look at her. But today he needs to forget his feelings for her and concentrate on defending the portal against her company's attack.

He takes the mic from Gus and asks Amanda, "When were you planning to tell the truth about why you're here?"

"I didn't lie. I am here to sell the Blue Moon."

"But the main reason you've come is to exploit our town for the benefit of your company!"

Amanda grabs the mic. "That's just not true. I'm here to help your town boost its economy. The income from the extra water and our company's increased presence will improve your community's standard of living. You can do good things with the extra money we bring to the table, like curing your serious pothole epidemic and paving all these unpaved roads."

"We happen to like our potholes and unpaved roads!" Chris insists.

"Nobody likes potholes!"

"We do!" Chris shouts.

Tom leans in toward the mic, trying to regain control. "What about the effect on the environment?"

Chris and Amanda are once again face-to-face, nose-to-nose, like they were in the street yesterday. But this time the mood is entirely different. They are both mad, and neither is giving an inch. Amanda is holding the microphone, but they are both talking directly into it.

"There will be little to no adverse effect," Amanda says.

"Rubbish! The DWA only cares about getting what it wants from us, which is more water they can sell to their customers, not helping us to keep what we have here intact. Somebody has to protect the environment from people like you and your big city bosses."

"Rubbish, yourself! You tree huggers give me a real

pain! You do more for yourselves than you ever do for the environment!"

Chris takes control of the mic. "Oh yeah? Like what? Saving an endangered species?"

"The DWA would never hurt an endangered species!"

"What about my family and our island then?"

Amanda retakes the microphone. "The Rainwaters represent an endangered species all on their own, then? Is that right?"

"I didn't say that."

Amanda speaks into the mic by herself. "That's ridiculous, unless you really are Bigfoot like Jack Newday thinks you are."

This comment gets the crowd's attention. Dinky, Sheriff Bob, Sam, and Clara all begin to cough and shuffle their feet as a light rain begins to fall. Amanda returns the mic to Tom, who says, "Weather is getting a bit dicey, folks. How about we call whatever this was a draw and head over to the island for the canoe race?"

Amanda leaves first, helped off the wagon by Jack. Chris follows and meets Francis below. Ebay has returned and stays right behind them as Chris and Francis make their way toward the town dock.

"Why is Jack's cat following us?" Chris asks Francis, who still harbors Bigfoot sniffer suspicions. Francis growls, turns, and chases Ebay into the crowd, barking.

Arriving at the town dock, Chris decides he can cross the lake faster if he doesn't go by boat. "I need to get to the island to check out my canoe, and I can get there faster if I swim," he says as Francis lopes up. "Keep your eyes open, and I'll see you at home later."

Francis opens his eyes extra wide but doesn't see Ebay crawling along the town pier. Out of sight of the crowd, Chris shapeshifts but is seen by Ebay, who then slips into a canoe and hides. Bigfoot Chris dives into the water and swims away. Ebay exits the canoe and slinks unseen by Francis toward Elk.

Cleo arrives at the dock after Chris has gone. She untethers her powerboat, steps in, starts her motor, and heads for the cove in front of the Blue Moon Inn. She eases up to the inn's dock as Jack and Amanda approach. Jack gets into the boat. Cleo suggests Amanda come with them to watch the canoe race. "It will be fun," she says.

"I'm not so sure," Amanda replies, still mad over her exchange with Chris at the parade. "I don't think I want to watch Chris Rainwater win at anything just now."

Jack interrupts, "Who said he's going to win? I have a feeling this is my year."

"Let's hope so," Amanda replies.

"I know Gabriel would be glad to see you," Cleo says to Amanda. "You could ask him about last night's blue moon. He knows more about that subject than anybody I know."

"I would like to see him again," Amanda says. "He was the closest to a grandfather I had when I was little."

She climbs aboard the Newday powerboat and takes a seat aft with Jack. At the wheel, Cleo points the nose of the craft toward the island and gives it the gas.

Chapter 25

Two Toots and We Have Winner

Good Bear Lake, Saturday

The rain worsens as the powerboat bumps slowly through the choppy water. Cleo is in front driving the boat, while Jack sits in the rear with Amanda under an umbrella. As they approach the Rainwater Island dock, Amanda stares at the rain falling on the surface of water and remembers the night her mother died, her falling into the water, and then seeing a large figure, obscured by the falling snow, swimming toward her.

Nearby, Bigfoot Chris swims through the waves and catches up to the powerboat from behind. As he overtakes the wooden craft, he sees Amanda is aboard, looking in his direction. He submerges and swims underwater, passing the powerboat as it approaches Rainwater Island dock. Arriving first, Bigfoot Chris changes into his human form underwater and gets out as Chris in his Bigfoot costume.

The powerboat thumps in, and Jack steps out, secures the boat, and helps Amanda onto the dock. They see Chris preparing his canoe for the upcoming race.

"How did he beat us here?" Amanda asks.

"Bigfoot is a really good swimmer, remember." Jack hands Amanda the umbrella, points to the steps, and suggests she watch the race from the top. She climbs the steps as the rain continues to fall.

At the dock, the race contestants gather, including Chris, Jack, Gus, Tom, Dinky, and Sam Summertime, with Chip still in his shirt pocket. They line up in their canoes. Cleo gets their attention, toots her air horn once, and informs the men of the rules: one toot of the horn and off they go, once around the island and back here to the starting line. "Two toots and we have a winner," she adds.

At the top of the steps, Amanda lowers her umbrella and steps under the covered porch at the rear of the barn. It has been more than twenty years since she was last on the island, and she has never seen the inside of the old barn. She drops her open umbrella on the porch and steps into the lightless space. She promptly bumps into a wooden bear. Backing away, she trips over a wooden fox kit, falls, and comes face-to-face with a wooden cougar.

Suddenly, the lights come on. Gabriel stands at the wall switch. "Don't worry, Amanda, they won't bite."

Amanda stands. "Dr. Rainwater. Thank goodness it's you."

"It's good to see you again, young lady. I heard you were in town."

"You remember me, then."

"I do. And your sweet mother." Gabriel hugs her. "Are you here for the race?"

She nods. "I came over with Cleo and Jack Newday. But mostly I came to see you." She hugs him back as a single air horn toot sounds outside.

"Sounds like they're off," Gabriel says.

Conditions on the water have not improved. The canoes struggle away from the starting line against the wind and blowing rain. Chris pulls away from the pack. Jack paddles himself into second place. Gus, Tom, and Dinky are a distant third, fourth, and fifth, with Sam bringing up the rear. Chip comes out of Sam's pocket with a tiny paddle and leans over the side. Trying to row, he falls into the lake. Sam turns his canoe and scoops the errant rodent out of the drink with his Summertime Hardware cap that reads, *Forever Summertime.*

"Don't help me, Chip. I'm doing badly enough as it is," he says. He squeezes the water from his gimme hat, puts it on, returns the soggy chipmunk to his pocket pouch, and retakes last place.

Inside the barn, Gabriel offers to show Amanda his workshop while they wait for the racers to return to this side of the island. As they pass under the limbs of the Douglas fir, Amanda notices the wooden birds perched high above.

"I understand those birds are carved from wood, but that tree looks real."

"That's because it is."

"How did you get a tree to grow in here?"

"The soil of this island is volcanic and very life-giving, especially below this barn."

"I see." She really doesn't, but she lets it go.

"Here's where I spend a good bit of my time these days," Gabriel says as he leads Amanda into his woodworking shop. He shows her the unfinished sign he's been working on, the one with the large-faced moon over a log structure.

"It reminds me of the inn and the big blue moon we had yesterday," she says. With her finger, she traces the carved moon. "Cleo says a blue moon can make people do funny things that they ordinarily might not."

"That's one theory. And then there's the school of thought that suggests a blue moon helps people do what deep in their hearts they would most like to do but have been afraid to."

"Which one is correct?"

"I'd have to say that depends on the person."

"How about someone like me?"

Gabriel looks at Amanda closely. "I'd say the jury is still out on you."

And he'd be right. The outcome of last night's escapade has served only to confuse Amanda's emotions rather than to clarify them.

"Eventually you'll have to decide that one for yourself," Gabriel adds and then leads her back into the barn.

"Thank you for showing me your workshop. That new sign is going to make someone very happy," Amanda says.

"It's a surprise for a very dear friend."

Out on the lake, the canoes have reached the halfway point. With great effort, Jack has closed the gap with Chris, and for a short time they are neck and neck. Chris surges and retakes the lead as they turn toward the finish line. It is a race now between Chris and Jack; none of the other contestants are close enough to challenge the two leaders.

Exiting the barn, Gabriel and Amanda again pass under the tree. Amanda notices the great horned owl is now on a limb very near the bottom. "Wasn't that owl higher up when we came in?"

"He was, but Who—that's his name—will do that."

"But how?"

Gabriel shrugs without responding.

Amanda notices the owl appears to be studying her. "Those big eyes of his make him look so real. Isn't he made of wood?"

"Most of the time, yes."

Amanda looks puzzled. "Your barn is an unusual place."

Gabriel smiles, dodges the implication, and replies, "We'd better hustle or we'll miss the end of the race."

Amanda and Gabriel leave the barn together and find that the rain has stopped. She closes the umbrella she left on the porch and looks back one last time at the peculiar old log structure with its long row of hand-blown rear windows and an owl inside named Who, who is wooden most of the time and moves from limb to limb in a tree that shouldn't be growing there in the first place. Very unusual. But even as a child, Amanda had recognized that Gabriel and his island were never what most people would have called usual.

She finally says, "I enjoyed hearing your thoughts about the blue moon. Though I'm still not sure how they apply to me."

"We'll just have to see then, won't we?"

"I guess so," Amanda replies, just as confused as she was when she arrived.

Below them, the canoes are approaching the finish line. "Oh, my goodness. Look at that," Gabriel says. "Jack is right there with Chris this year. It's going to be close."

Cleo waits on the dock, air horn at the ready. From his canoe, Chris sees Amanda and Gabriel on the steps above. Jack is closing in from behind. Chris continues to look up at Amanda and Gabriel. Not paying attention, he paddles off course and crashes into the dock. Jack holds his line and crosses the finish first. Cleo hits her horn. *Toot, toot.* Jack is the winner.

On the hilltop, Gabriel says to Amanda, "Looks like the town's got itself a new Bigfoot next year."

Chapter 26

Barring Something Drastic

All Are Welcome Church, Saturday

Like most of the town of Good Bear Lake, Rev. Dinky Round Rock's All-Are-Welcome nondenominational Church is late nineteenth century Victorian in design. It has a single steeple with a bell, and this afternoon, Jack's red pickup is parked out front. Cleo's voice can be heard coming from the inside, rehearsing her wedding solo: "*Joyful, joyful, we adore Thee, God of Glory, Lord of Love …*"

Inside the empty church, sitting in a pew near the front, Jack looks at his mother and touches his watch, indicating he is out of time.

"*Hearts unfold like flowers before Thee, opening to the sun above,*" Cleo sings and then speaks to her piano player, Becky Proudlow. "Hey, Beck, how about we take a little break?"

"Back in five." Becky stands, nods at Jack, and passes up the center aisle toward the rear of the small church.

Cleo hands Jack his lunch box. "There's an extra package of Twinkies inside," she says.

"Thanks, Mom."

"Let me ask you something."

"Okay."

"Why don't you just leave Chris alone?"

"Because I'm trying to show people who he really is."

Cleo shakes her head. "Barring something drastic, son, no one in this town is going to change how they think about someone they've known their whole lives."

Cleo moves back to the piano. Jack's face shines as if he's had an epiphany, and he says to himself, "Barring something drastic." He takes out his cell phone and calls Gus Cobb.

Driving in his pickup along the dusty shoreline road toward the new tunnel, Gus answers Jack's call. Amanda sits on the front seat beside Gus as he makes a deal to show Jack their operation. Gus asks Amanda to stay for Jack's visit, and she agrees.

"How are things going with Cleo?" he asks as they turn onto the gravel road that leads onto the DWA work site.

"I'm having trouble getting her to hold still long enough to talk to her."

"Like I told you, that woman's as slippery as Coal Creek Alley after a big snow."

"Now she's all wound up with Chris's wedding."

"What do you think about Chris getting married?"

"I think it's none of my business," she says. She would like to have said, "I hate the thought of Chris getting married." But she knew she shouldn't, and so, she didn't.

"I got the feeling from watching you two at the parade this morning there might be something more going on between you. Then there was the rehearsal dinner incident last night everybody was talking about this morning."

"What happened to us last night was caused by the blue moon."

"How does that work?"

"I'm not really sure. But can we not talk about this right

now?" She has been feeling bad enough, and now she is feeling even worse.

"When, then? Chris is getting married in a few hours."

"I guess that means never," Amanda replies and points at Jack's truck sitting in front of the work trailer by the opening to the new tunnel, which is directly above the old tunnel below the waterline. "Jack is already here."

Inside the trailer, Gus shows Amanda and Jack a map of the new bore. "We're on hold right now awaiting the final concreting of the walls and the ceiling, pending the city council's approval."

"Which hopefully should come sooner rather than later," Amanda says.

"Let's go see," Gus adds, handing out hard hats and leading Amanda and Jack toward the new tunnel's opening.

Inside the tunnel, naked bulbs hang from the ceiling, lighting their way. Call boxes are spaced along the walls with walkie-talkies inside. Gus explains that the mobile transmitters are used to contact the working crew on the Denver side since their cell phones don't work underground.

"How about it, Gus? Can we go see the pumping station next?" Jack asks.

"Tell you what," Amanda says to Jack. "Why don't I drive Gus's truck back to town so I can run your mother down and maybe get her to hold still for a change? You and Gus can drive over to the pumping station in your pickup."

Jack agrees and goes after his truck. "See you out front in a bit, Gus."

Amanda and Gus exit together. She pats the wall. "Looks like you all are just about done."

"Close, but not totally. If the level of the lake were to rise now and suddenly fill the new bore with water before it has its concrete covering in place, the strain could result in the walls shifting and could collapse the ceiling."

Gus and Jack take the lakeshore road to the pumping station near the dam. The pumping station controls the pumps that move water from the Shadow Mountain Reservoir up to the lake to maintain a constant water level. The station also runs the spillway sluices by which water can be drained from the lake down into the reservoir when required.

"The sluices can also be opened manually by turning that thing." Gus points out the great metal wheel to Jack as they pass by.

"Wouldn't something like that be hard to turn by hand?" Jack asks.

"Impossible for one man. It would take a crew of pretty strong fellows to get that monster moving."

"I'll bet Bigfoot could do it."

"Maybe if he had a strong friend or two with him," Gus says, smiling.

Jack pulls into the lot in front of the pumping station and cuts off his truck motor. "Let's go have a look inside."

Inside the main room of the pumping station, they study the control panel.

"How much water would it take to flood the island?" Jack asks.

"Oh, eight or so hours of continuous flow with all four pumps running at maximum should do it," Gus replies.

"And which button controls the spillway sluices that drain water out of the lake?"

Gus touches the big red button at the bottom of the panel. "This fellow here."

"I see, there at the bottom." He'll need to remember that.

"That's the one. Hey, listen," Gus says, "we should get going. I've got a good bit of work left to do at the office before the wedding." He closes the panel and the two men return to the front of the station.

"Wouldn't want to be late for the wedding," Jack says, holding the door open for Gus. Jack exits last.

Gus walks toward Jack's pickup. "Hey, Jack, pull the door closed behind you, will you?"

"Will do." Jack waves and takes a plastic credit card from his wallet, uses it to block the lock, and follows Gus to his pickup. "No worries. She's locked up tight," he shouts.

Chapter 27

Skunks Have More Going for Them than You Might Think

Blue Moon Inn, Saturday

Amanda walks in from town and sees Chris waiting for her on the porch of the inn. She picks up the broken sign out front, blown completely off its hinges by today's wind. Chris comes to help her. Together they carry the heavy wooden sign toward the porch. The mood has again changed. The flare-up at the parade is over. Once again, Chris is back to that good feeling he gets when he's with her. But then, as usual, neither of them says what they are really thinking.

Chris begins, "I just came by to tell you I was sorry for how I acted at the parade. I know you're just trying to do your job, even though I don't agree with what your company is doing."

"I'm sorry about what happened to us at the parade, too. But especially for our behavior at the rehearsal dinner last night."

"As am I," Chris adds. Although, he is only sorry about their fight at the parade. He enjoyed himself at the rehearsal, particularly during the last part of the evening, the "you may kiss your bride" part. Yet, he knows nothing has changed. He can't allow himself to believe in a love that can never be. They are still worlds apart.

"Cleo blames what we did on the blue moon," Amanda says, remembering last night's kiss and how good it had made her feel. Not just schoolgirl good but grown-up woman good. Which is it? Did the blue moon make her do it? Or did she do it because deep down inside she wanted to? She has no idea.

"Same thing Lulu says," Chris replies.

"The wedding's still on, then?" She wishes it weren't. But she says nothing.

"It is." Chris also wishes it weren't. But he knows there's too much at stake. And he says nothing.

They look at each other with regret in their eyes. They arrive at the steps and prop the broken sign against the side of the porch.

"Lulu's the greatest," Chris says. And she surely is. But he doesn't love her.

"That's what I hear," Amanda replies and wishes Lulu, admittedly the greatest, lived elsewhere, somewhere far away elsewhere.

They climb the stairs and sit on the same top step from so long ago. Amanda recalls the night Chris refused to take her hand. She still hurts from that rebuke, even after all this time. What could have made him withdraw from her when she needed his support so badly?

While sweeping the deck next door at the marina, Cleo looks at the inn and sees Chris and Amanda sitting on the front porch together. Promising scenario. She drops the broom and takes off through the aspens for the inn on foot. To hear what the two are saying to each other, she's going to have to sneak under the front steps. Unphased by the nefarious prospect, Cleo comes out of the trees, gets onto all fours, and crawls beneath the porch.

On the top step, a few feet from the closed-eyed, leafless aspen trees of Jane James's Gabriel-carved front door, Amanda admits to Chris she should have told him right away who she worked for. And Chris tells her that he would have liked to have been able to be more honest with her about himself. But the aspens' eyes stay closed and the limbs remain leafless.

"What do you mean?"

"I can't tell you. Not without permission."

"Whose permission?" she asks.

"I can't tell you that either." And he can't.

"I don't get it." And she doesn't.

Beneath the porch, Cleo notices that the skunk from town is sitting beside her with his ears perked up. Like her, he is listening to Chris and Amanda stumble through their awkwardness.

"Gabriel? Is that you?" she whispers to the eavesdropping skunk.

The skunk nods, yes. This meeting between Chris and Amanda is clearly going no place.

Again, Cleo whispers to the skunk, "What do you think?"

The skunk makes a dissatisfied blowing sound with his skunky lips. "*Phooey.*"

Amanda hears the skunky noise from under the porch steps. "I'm getting more and more confused," she says. And she is. And the situation isn't getting any better. Not today, at least.

"I know, and I'm sorry," Chris says and stands, looking at his watch. He's going to be marrying Lulu very soon, so what is he doing here with Amanda on her front porch, wanting to—but trying not to—say things he knows he can't say?

"I guess you'd better get going. Wouldn't want to be late to your own wedding, would you?" Amanda says, though she really doesn't mean it.

"No. I guess not," Chris replies. But he doesn't need to guess. He knows he doesn't mean it. He would prefer to stay here with Amanda rather than to go anywhere, especially not to this wedding with Lulu.

Under the porch, the skunk looks at Cleo, shakes his black-and-white V-striped head, and takes off as Chris descends the steps above them. Cleo follows the skunk from under the porch and watches him scurry unseen behind Chris and down the single-track trail toward his canoe.

Through the empty trees, Amanda watches Chris climb into his canoe and then the skunk sneak aboard and slip under the tarp in back.

Cleo suddenly appears.

"Did you see that?" Amanda says to her.

"Uh-huh," Cleo says.

"Don't you think that's strange?"

"Not as strange as two people who need to talk saying nothing that means anything with the clock ticking."

"Was that you I heard underneath the porch just now?"

"Yes. And we were very disappointed."

"We?"

"Me," Cleo says and points as the skunk peeks out from under the canoe's tarp, "and him."

"But he's a skunk," Amanda says.

"Skunks have more going for them than you might think."

As Chris paddles away, the skunk looks back at the two women, sticks out his skunk-red tongue, and mimes another fat *phooey.*

Amanda blinks. "Apparently so."

Chapter 28

Like I Said Before

Blue Moon Inn, Saturday

From her mother's old bedroom, Amanda looks out the win-dow at Rainwater Island, lit by an early yellow moon. The wardrobe stands open, and her suitcase sits on a chair. She packs her DWA jacket and then takes her mother's old sweater from the wardrobe and lovingly brushes it off. She puts it on and goes back to the window. The tree lights on the city hall lawn are glowing blue in the clear night sky, and the bell in the tower of the All Are Welcome Church is ringing, announcing that Chris and Lulu's wedding is about to take place inside. Amanda isn't going.

At the church, the parking lot is filled with cars, pickup trucks, bicycles, and a pair of horses tied to the bike rack. The yellow moon seems to be sitting directly above the spire of the old church as the bell rings the last of the guests inside. Cleo's voice can be heard finishing her solo: "*Ever singing, march we forward, victors in the midst of strife, joyful music leads us sunward, in the triumph song of life.*"

Minutes later, Becky plays "*Here Comes the Bride*" on the piano. At the altar stands Chris with Francis at his leg and Gabriel by his side as Sheriff Bob and Lulu arrive, her arm through his. When Becky concludes her traditional wedding entrance music, Rev. Round Rock starts the ceremony.

The pews in front contain familiar faces. Lyle and Ruthie, holding their new baby boy, sit in the front row with the other three Firths spread across the long bench beside their parents. Sam and Clara Summertime, with Chip safely tucked into Sam's front shirt pocket, are just behind them.

When Sam leans forward to replace his hymnal in the tray on the back of the pew in front of him, Chip falls from his pocket into Clara's open purse on the floor, which she then picks up and places on the seat cushion beside her. She zips the noisy, tool-filled purse closed, unaware that Chip is inside.

Shoo flies from the rafters and lands on the Summertime's pew in front of Gus. He looks Gus in the eye. Neither man nor bird blink—a sacramental truce of sorts.

At the altar, Dinky moves quickly through the ritual, taking no chances, and is getting close to the end. "Any man who knows why Chris and Lulu should not be joined in matrimony, let him speak now or forever hold his peace," he says.

He takes a big breath and holds it. Francis leaves Chris's side and moves next to Gabriel. Francis and Gabriel look at each other and then at Dinky. Francis barks, but Gabriel shushes him and says nothing. Dinky looks sharply at Francis. Francis hushes, settles back, and crouches beside Chris.

Lulu and Cleo turn toward Jack, who sits quietly in the last row of the church. As they turn back to the front, Ebay appears in the aisle and jumps onto Jack's lap. Jack calmly strokes his cat and says nothing.

Dinky finally exhales. "I now pronounce you man and wife," he says, the relief in his voice palpable, and closes his book. "You may kiss your bride."

Chris does but this time only a peck, nothing like last night's glorious kiss under the influence of the blue moon. Tonight's moon, like Chris's mood, is a mellow yellow.

Becky plays the recessional hymn, and Chris and Lulu exit up the center aisle. As they pass Jack, he whispers into Ebay's ear. "Like I said before, cat, this ain't over yet."

Chapter 29

He's Got an Idea

All Are Welcome Church, Saturday

The wedding reception is taking place in the garden at the side of the church and is winding down. Clara Summertime puts her purse on the end of the food table, opens it, and removes her handkerchief. While she's blowing her nose, Chip climbs out and breaks off a chunk of a Ruthie blueberry muffin. As is his habit, he begins to wander as he eats and walks off the end of the table. Shoo darts down from a tree limb above the gathering and catches the falling chipmunk in midair. He then drops Chip inside Clara's open purse and spears the half-eaten muffin fragment.

Without looking, Clara covers Chip with her handkerchief and zips her purse closed. Trapped again. Shoo returns to his perch on the limb to enjoy the reward of his daring midair rescue.

Outside the garden bathroom off the back of the church, Francis nudges Gabriel's leg and waves at Shoo with his paw. He wants to talk. Gabriel and Francis enter the bathroom as Shoo, the muffin thief, flies in through the high open window. Gabriel remains in his human form, while the other two change into their respective larger and more verbal Bigfoot personae, overfilling the small space.

"We've got to stop this honeymoon," Bigfoot Francis says.

"I agree," Gabriel replies.

"He agrees," Bigfoot Shoo says.

Outside, Gus, hearing voices, rattles the knob. "Anybody in there?"

"Be right out," Gabriel says from inside.

"Be right out," Bigfoot Shoo repeats, to no one's surprise.

Outside, Gus scratches his bald head and looks perplexed.

Inside the small overloaded space, the threesome puts their heads together.

"What do we do now?" Bigfoot Francis whispers.

"I've got an idea," Gabriel says.

"He's got an—" Bigfoot Francis stifles Bigfoot Shoo with a furry hand.

Outside, Gus hears the toilet flush. The door opens and out comes Gabriel.

"Sorry to be so slow, Gus," he says.

"That's fine, Gabriel, no hurries," Gus replies.

Francis emerges as a dog with Shoo, a bird again, riding on his back. Shoo winks at Gus. Gus goes inside the bathroom, looks in the mirror, and again scratches his shiny head.

In the garden, Chris and Lulu are helping with the cleanup. They tip a table onto its side to close the legs.

"Looks like it might snow," Lulu says.

"Plenty of blankets on the island," Chris replies.

"Is that where we're going to, you know ...?"

"Yeah. Gabriel's letting us use his big bedroom upstairs."

"With the one with the big four-poster bed and its own bathroom? That's great, but where will Gabriel sleep?"

"In my room or more likely on the couch by the fireplace next to Francis's bed. He often does that anyway on chilly nights. It's Francis that's got me worried," Chris says as a screw drops out of the hinge on the table leg. Chris picks it up and waves the Summertimes over. "Clara, you wouldn't happen to have a screwdriver in that purse of yours, would you?"

"You want to bet?" Sam says.

Clara sets her purse on the food table and opens it. Chip climbs out holding three screwdrivers—one slot head, one Phillips head, and one Allen head—circled by his short chipmunk arms. He points the heads at Chris for selection.

Chris checks the missing screw and choses the slot head. "Boy," he says to Clara, "you nuts-and-bolts guys don't miss a trick."

Sam reaches down and picks Chip up. "There you are. We've been wondering where you got off to," he says to the errant rodent and offers him a bite of Clara's banana nut bread. Chip looks askance at Clara, who has zipped him up in her purse. Twice.

"Sorry," Clara says.

Chip finally accepts the banana bread offering and takes a small bite. He then climbs, still munching the somewhat overdone pastry, into Sam's hand for the return trip to his pocket.

As Chris replaces the lost screw in the table hinge, Lulu says, "Anyway, Francis says they aren't coming over until after you and I have gotten squared away upstairs, which I thought was nice of him."

"Francis, being nice. Now that is worrisome," Chris says.

Chapter 30

What Is that Smell?

Good Bear Lake, Saturday

At the town dock, Chris loads Lulu's suitcase into his canoe. Neither he nor Lulu see Shoo sneak out from under the tarp, stab the drain plug with his beak, pull it out, and fly away. Water immediately bubbles into the bottom of their canoe. In the middle of the lake, Chris paddles like crazy while Lulu bails water from their fast-filling boat with her cupped hands.

As they near the island dock, the canoe sinks. Chris swims for Lulu's suitcase before it can disappear below the surface. They struggle out of the lake and onto the dock. Chris carries Lulu's suitcase over his head as they slosh up the steps toward the house.

"I don't get it. We take such good care of our boats," he says to Lulu.

"Accidents happen," she replies.

Chris looks around. "Accidents, huh?"

Wet and cold, Chris and Lulu approach the house, dripping as they go.

"Where did Francis say he was going after the reception?" Chris asks.

"He didn't."

Unseen, Bigfoot Francis and Gabriel exit their overstuffed canoe at the dock. Shoo flies in and changes into his Bigfoot form. Gabriel and the two Bigfoot boys wait below as Chris and Lulu enter the house.

"Okay," Bigfoot Francis says to Bigfoot Shoo. "You know what to do."

"Know what to do," Bigfoot Shoo repeats.

"After Chris leaves the bathroom, you fly in and cut the light back on."

"Cut the light back on."

"But be sure he doesn't see you."

"Who?"

"Chris."

"Right. Chris doesn't see me."

"We don't want him to know you did it."

"Did what?"

"Cut the light back on."

"Right. The light back on."

"Then you fly out the window and stay out of sight."

"Out of sight. Got it."

"Here we go," Gabriel says, and they all change forms. Gabriel goes to a skunk, Francis to a dog, and Shoo to a bird. They start up the steps, the skunk in the lead.

Inside the house, Chris stacks the wood and lights the fireplace. Lulu takes a seat by the fire as Chris leaves for the back of the house, intending to dry Lulu's things in the dryer, which like the oven, doesn't turn on.

"The dryer doesn't work and neither does the oven!" he shouts to Lulu in the great room.

He tries the hot water faucet in the kitchen. Nothing there either. Chris is unsure enough about this evening already, with a leaky boat and a soaking wet bride, and now this.

"No hot water either!" he shouts.

Lulu pulls the blanket around her shoulders and edges closer to the flames. "Don't worry. We can dry by the fire."

Chris comes in. "First, it's the drain plug and the dryer. Then the oven. And now it's the water heater. There's something very fishy going on around here."

He glances out the window and sees Shoo fly by. He opens the window and shouts into the darkness: "It's a good thing you can't break a fireplace!"

"What's going on?" Lulu asks.

"The boys are up to something."

Later, Chris, dressed in his pajamas, cleans his teeth in the upstairs bathroom that connects to Gabriel's big bedroom on the second floor. He lowers the window but leaves it partially open and switches off the lights. The room goes black. He enters the bedroom, hurries to bed in the dark, and hops in beside Lulu.

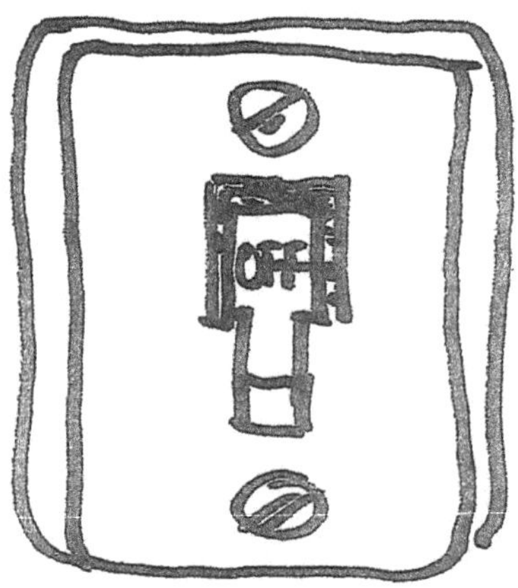

"It's freezing out there," he says.

"Feels great in here," Lulu says as the light in the bathroom comes on.

"That's funny," Chris says. He hustles to the bathroom, cuts off the light again and returns. He jumps into the big four poster bed with the herd of elk carved on the face of its broad headboard and drags up the covers.

"What was it?" Lulu asks.

"You got me."

The bathroom light comes on.

"Now what?" Chris says.

Lulu gets up. "Let me this time."

Lulu enters the bathroom, looks around, sees nothing, switches off the light, and heads for the bed. As she climbs in, the light comes on.

"That's strange," she says.

"I think I know what's going on," Chris says.

Several moments later in the bathroom, Lulu switches off the light and leaves. Shoo comes out from behind the shower curtain and turns on the light with his beak. Chris jumps out from behind the door and grabs him.

"I don't blame you, Shoo. I know who's behind this." He opens the window, releases Shoo into the night, and shouts. "Francis! That's right, Francis. Not Frank. You're a dog, and you're going to be a dead one if you don't cut this out!"

The skunk, followed by Francis and Shoo, come quietly up the wooden steps from the great room and pause in the hall outside the big bedroom, listening. All quiet inside. They slip through the doorway and sneak under the bed just as Chris makes his way into the room.

"That should do it," Chris says and again climbs under the covers.

Lulu starts sniffing. "My God!"

"What is that smell?" Chris shouts.

Chapter 31

Look Out for that Twinkie

Pumping Station, Saturday

With Ebay at his side, Jack sits in his truck outside the pump-ing station, thinking. It's time for action, drastic action. The wedding has ended, and the honeymoon has begun. Lulu is the bride, but Jack is not the groom. He realizes his mother is avoiding the question as to why she won't change her vote, and he can no longer look to her for help. It's up to him to flush Bigfoot from his hiding place on the island, to handle things in his own way for the good of the town, and to save Lulu before it's too late. He puts his hand on his bow, which hangs behind him on the rear window rack, and picks up his lunch box.

"Come on, Ebay. It's up to us now," he says. He exits his truck, goes to the pumping station door, and removes the plastic card he used to block the lock earlier. Followed by Ebay, he enters the building and locates the control panel. He sits down, opens his lunch box, and removes a pair of wire clippers, a screwdriver, and a half-eaten package of Twinkies. He pushes the button to activate the pumps, which whir immediately on.

"Drastic enough?" he asks Ebay.

Water is now moving from the reservoir below into the lake. The only task left is to destroy the connection to the emergency spillway so that no one can undo what he is doing. He opens the panel with his screwdriver.

The only other way to reverse the flow is by turning the massive metal wheel manually—not humanly possible but very likely the place where Jack suspects he will find Bigfoot Chris when he tries to open the spillway to save the island. Jack plans to be there.

He takes out his clippers and prepares to cut the wire to the spillway control button.

"Watch out for the Twinkie!" he shouts at Ebay, who is walking across the control panel.

The startled feline jumps instead onto the half-eaten snack. Sticky white goo from inside squirts across the board. Sparks fly, and the whole panel goes black. Jack presses the big red sluice-control button. Nothing happens. There is no sound except that of the pump motors whirring outside. He goes to the window and looks out. Water is still flooding into the lake from the four large pipes on the hillside above the waterline. The spillway sluices remain closed. Ebay's accident has shorted out the entire spillway system.

He picks Ebay up and strokes her head. "Good job, Ebay. Never would have thought of that."

Chapter 32

The Second One Is a Dog

Rainwater Island, Sunday

Shoo flies around the great room, squawking. Gabriel comes out from under his blanket, coughing. He is lying on the couch in front of a smoldering fire in the fireplace. Francis is in his bed at Gabriel's feet.

"Francis. See what's got Shoo so worked up."

Outside the house, the lake level has risen overnight. Water threatens not only the house but also the barn with the portal inside. Francis steps out the front door and falls into the water. Chris is next to exit the house, with Shoo on his arm. With Francis's help, he reaches a canoe floating by, pulls it to the porch, and ties it off.

A short distance away, with Ebay at his side, Jack sits in his own boat. He is watching the front door of the Rainwater house through binoculars. He focuses on Chris.

"We've got him now, cat. All we have to do is stay close and wait for him to show himself for who he really is at the spillway." Jack touches his camera case and his bow and quiver. "And be ready to end this once and for all."

Gabriel comes onto the porch and says to Chris and the boys, "Someone must have turned on the reservoir pumps last night. You three will have to make sure they are off and then open the spillway sluices to drain the extra water back into the reservoir before the barn floods."

"We understand, Grandfather," Chris says, and Francis and Shoo nod.

Lulu comes onto the porch. "What's happening?"

"Someone switched on the pumps last night and moved water from the reservoir into the lake," Chris tells her.

"Start with the pumping station," Gabriel says to Chris, "and remember there's always the manual spillway wheel at the dam. You and Francis should be able to turn it, but you'll probably have to work together to get it to move."

"Yes, Grandfather," Chris says and then speaks to Shoo. "Stay over the lake and keep your eyes open. I suspect Jack is behind this, and he may be watching us even now. If you spot him following us, let me know."

Shoo squawks his understanding, opens his broad wings, and is swept aloft by a gust of wind into the morning November breeze.

"You think it was Jack, then?" Lulu affirms.

"That would be my guess, yes." Chris gets in the canoe and helps Lulu aboard. Francis follows Lulu in.

Chris and Lulu paddle away from the house, which, like the barn, remains above the waterline. Time is against them. The barn will be collecting water soon unless the pumps are halted and the spillway sluices are opened. It's up to Chris and the boys to reverse the flow.

Shoo flies above the lake. Chris and Lulu, with Francis between them, paddle their canoe, heading for the town dock. A second canoe follows not far behind. Shoo swoops and buzzes the second boat. He hovers eye to eye with Ebay and then with Jack, the paddler. Shoo has a quick go at the drain plug but can't budge it. Looking around the canoe, he sees the camera and the bow and quiver.

"Shoo," Jack says to the jaybird and takes a swing at him with his paddle. He misses.

Shoo flies away, squawking at Jack in a language Jack doesn't understand.

Across the lake at the Blue Moon Inn, Amanda is dressing in the upstairs bedroom. She hears a knock. She opens the door to find Cleo in the hall. "What's going on?" she asks.

"Better come see for yourself."

They go to the landing above the stairs. Tom Throttle is in the great room below them, floating in a canoe. The entire lower floor of the inn is underwater. Cleo tells Amanda it's the same at the marina.

"What's going on?" Amanda asks.

Cleo tells her the lake level is up, way up.

Tom adds, "Gus says somebody broke into the pump station last night and moved water from the reservoir into the lake. DWA's new tunnel and the two waterfront properties, the marina and the inn, are already flooding, and the island isn't far behind."

Amanda and Cleo descend the stairs and step aboard Tom's canoe.

"Then whoever it was shorted out the emergency spillway circuit using some sort of sticky, white, gooey substance," Tom says.

Cleo raises her eyebrows. Sticky, white, gooey substance sounds familiar.

Tom and Cleo paddle Amanda out the front door of the inn and toward Tom's truck, which is parked above the waterline.

"What do we do now?" Amanda asks.

"Gus called and asked me to let the Denver side crew know

what's happened here and that the new tunnel is filling with water. Time is of the essence before their part of the tunnel becomes dangerous too, with the increasing water pressure. He says to try the wall transmitters but to be careful."

"Why doesn't Gus call someone in his crew?"

"His men are all out of town, waiting for the council to change their vote before they can return to work. Gus is alone here, and he's gone to the pumping station to try to get the system up and running. He already has the pumps off, but he still can't get the spillway motors to work."

Amanda has a thought. "I've been inside the new tunnel. I know where the wall boxes with the transmitters are, and I can hold the flashlight while you paddle."

"That would be a big help, but Gus says we should move fast before the water level gets too high inside the tunnel."

Upon arriving at the town dock, Lulu exits Chris's canoe.

"Have your dad let everyone at the hall know about the danger to the portal," Chris says.

"Will do. Where are you and Francis going?"

"To reverse the water flow."

In his canoe, Jack watches through his binoculars as Lulu leaves and Chris remains behind in his canoe with Francis. Chris shapeshifts into Bigfoot Chris.

"Lulu, you poor thing," Jack says to Ebay. Then he watches Francis change form and become Bigfoot Francis. Jack lowers his binoculars. "Holy cow. There's two of them, and one is a dog. How could I have overlooked something like that?"

If Francis were a regular dog, Jack realizes, he would be well over thirty by now and not in doggy years. Not only is that not likely, it's not possible. After a moment, Jack decides that, but for a canine Bigfoot, it's probably no big deal.

"Mother has been right all along," he says to Ebay. "It is complicated."

Jack paddles hard. He is no match for the two strong-armed Bigfoot paddlers. However, he knows where they are headed. He can take his time. He puts his camera case and his bow and quiver at his feet, where he can easily reach them, and continues to paddle toward the spillway sluices.

Bigfoot Chris and Bigfoot Francis paddle at double Bigfoot speed across the lake. Nearing the pumping station, they change forms into human and dog, dock their canoe, and get out. Gus exits the station and waves them over.

Chris talks, with Francis looking on. "How's it going?" he asks Gus.

"The pumps are off, but the spillway connection is fried."

"What about opening the spillway sluices manually by turning the wheel?"

"That would do it, yes, but that wheel is too big and too rusty to be turned by one or even two men alone," Gus says.

"But if it could be turned, then the water would drain into the reservoir, right?" Chris asks.

"That's correct. But I'm not sure an entire crew of men could manage it. That manual wheel hasn't been used in several years."

Shoo lands on Chris's shoulder and whispers in his ear. Chris says, "You're sure it's Jack?" Shoo nods. "And he has his camera with him?" Shoo nods again. "And his bow?" And yes, yet again.

Gus notices Chris's banter with the whispering jaybird. A nod followed by a pair of nods. Shoo and Gus look at each other briefly. Shoo nods a fourth yes, this time at Gus, who continues, "If … uh… the wheel could be turned, then the water level would drop fast." He turns and points to the big iron wheel above the dam. "It's just that it's not humanly possible."

Gus turns to find Chris and Francis are gone. Shoo rises in the air and circles Gus a time or two as Chris and Francis race for their canoe. Shoo then flies away. Unseen by Gus, Chris and Francis change into their Bigfoot forms and paddle toward the dam and the sticky spillway wheel. Jack, once again, is nowhere in sight.

Chapter 33

His Aim to the Right

New DWA tunnel, Sunday.

The new bore is rapidly filling with water. With Amanda as a passenger, Tom paddles his canoe into its mouth. Flashlight in hand, Amanda scans the walls and remembers what Gus said about the increasing water pressure against the unconcreted walls. Finally, she locates a transmitter with the light. Tom retrieves the walkie-talkie from the box and switches to send mode.

"Hello, the other side." There is no response. "Hello, anybody there?" he repeats as a loud crack is heard above them.

Tom looks up. The ceiling is breaking up.

"Let's get out of here!" he shouts.

Suddenly, large blocks of rock begin to fall as the ceiling collapses, creating a massive wave that tosses Tom and Amanda into the water. The new tunnel is imploding from the increasing water pressure on the unconcreted walls, as Gus suggested it might. Tom is swept to safety by the surge, but Amanda is left inside, trapped. As chunks of large rock splash around her, she clings to Tom's capsized canoe in the dark without the flashlight and shivering from the cold.

Chris and Francis, in their Bigfoot forms, beach their

canoe and approach the big metal wheel above the dam nearby the pumping station. In his canoe, Jack is already there and readies his camera to photograph the expected event. He takes picture after picture of the action as Bigfoot Chris tries alone to turn the wheel but can't. Bigfoot Francis moves to help, and together they strain to budge it. The rusted metal seal cracks and then breaks. The old wheel groans and begins to turn. The emergency sluices are now open. Water pours from the lake into the reservoir below.

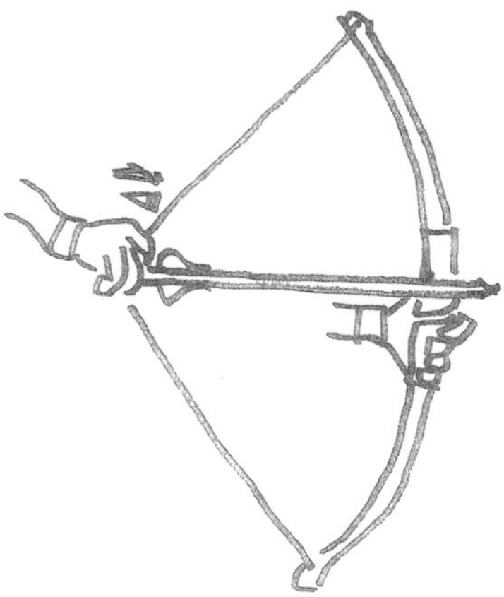

Less than twenty yards from shore, Jack puts his camera in its case and picks up his bow. Shoo swoops from the sky and tries to steal the camera. Jack waves Shoo away with his bow.

"No, you don't. Not this time," he says and nocks an arrow. At this range, Jack knows he can easily hit the heart. It's very nearly the same shot he made on Friday at the stationhouse.

As he draws his bow and readies himself to turn loose the arrow, he feels a presence behind him and then a hand on his right shoulder. He shifts his aim to the right and releases the bow string. The arrow flies over the water and strikes Bigfoot Chris, not in his heart but in his right shoulder. Jarred backward, Bigfoot Chris drops to his knees.

Jack looks behind him in the canoe but sees no one. He searches the calm water, but again, there is nothing. He had an easy kill shot and then did not make it. He has no idea why or who might have touched his shoulder. He turns his attention to the wounded Bigfoot Chris on shore.

"At least that should slow you down, Mr. Bigfoot!" he shouts and then puts down his bow and looks around one more time. Clearly, he is alone. He picks up his paddle and rows for the marina.

Bigfoot Francis pulls the arrow from Bigfoot Chris's shoulder.

"What do we do now, Chris?"

"Take me to Gabriel," Bigfoot Chris replies.

Bigfoot Francis helps him into their canoe and steers it toward the island.

"I don't understand how Jack could have missed. He's a dead shot at that range," Bigfoot Chris says.

"He's been after you so long, maybe he got excited," Bigfoot Francis says. "Or maybe a wave hit his canoe?"

"Or maybe he missed on purpose."

"Why would he do that?"

"I don't know. We'll ask Gabriel."

By the time they arrive at the island, Chris and Francis are human and dog again. Gabriel is waiting for them on the barn porch. The water level is receding, and the portal is safe.

"What happened?" Gabriel asks.

"Jack shot me in the shoulder with an arrow." Chris shows Gabriel his wound. "He could have easily killed me, but he didn't. And I don't know why."

"Was there anyone with him?" Gabriel says.

"Not that I could see."

"Ah, no one visible, then." He hesitates and then adds, "So, it begins."

"What begins?"

"I'll explain later. Right now, Amanda is in trouble." He tells Chris the news, that Amanda is trapped inside the new tunnel. Gus has called in his crew and they are trying to get her out, but they may not be able to get to her in time. She is in grave danger.

Chris knows he must be sure that Amanda is safe, no matter the risk to himself. "I have to save her, Grandfather."

"I understand, Chris. But before you go, let's get you up to Bigfoot speed."

Gabriel leads Chris into the barn and onto the steps to the portal. At the bottom, Gabriel takes his Bigfoot form and puts his left hand on the door, which turns faintly blue. He then places his right hand, the side with the leather wristband, on Chris's shoulder wound.

After removing his hand, he reverts to his human self. "How does that feel?"

The wound has healed. Chris puts his shoulder through a range of motion. "Fine now, Grandfather. Thank you."

"Be careful, Chris."

"I'll do my best."

"I know, Chris. And take the boys with you. I'll let Bob Big Sky know to watch out for you and to help in any way he can."

Chapter 34

Are You Bigfoot?

New DWA tunnel, Sunday.

In addition to Gus's crew, which is working to free Amanda, the crisis in the tunnel has attracted media reporters from Denver.

Though the water has started to recede, it still fills most of the new bore. At the mouth of the tunnel, a female reporter speaks in front of a TV camera: "Earlier today, Amanda James of the Denver Water Authority was trapped inside the new tunnel at Good Bear Lake. All efforts to rescue the young woman so far have failed," she says into her microphone.

Inside the work trailer, Gus, Chris, and Francis study a map of the two tunnels. Francis points to a place on the map with his paw. Shoo flies in through the window, walks around on the map, and after a moment pecks the same spot with his beak.

"What about that shaft there?" Chris asks Gus, indicating the location Francis and Shoo have selected.

Gus looks at Shoo and Francis, and then he responds, "It does connect the new bore with the old main tunnel, but with the lake level up, it will be full of water too."

Shoo squawks and makes a swimming motion with his

wings. Chris and Francis nod at each other as if to say, good suggestion.

"Couldn't someone swim through the old tunnel and use that cross shaft to enter the new one?"

"Yes. If they could hold their breath long enough and then have the strength left to open the metal hatch between the two tunnels," Gus says, watching Francis rummage through his toolbox. "It's just not possible," he adds.

"Like turning the spillway wheel by hand wasn't possible?"

"Exactly. By the way, how did you do that?" Gus asks.

"Francis helped quite a bit."

Gus looks at Francis again. The big dog turns with a waterproof flashlight in his mouth and winks. Gus flinches and says, "Right, right."

Shoo squawks loudly and then a second later squawks again: jaybird for "right, right."

Outside at the entrance to the tunnel, the media crowd mills about, waiting for something to happen. Tom, Cleo, and Sheriff Bob Big Sky watch Chris hurry past them without speaking. Francis is step for step behind Chris, holding the waterproof flashlight in his mouth.

"Where's Chris going in such a hurry?" Tom says.

"To save Amanda," Cleo replies.

"But what can he do?"

Shoo dives at a cameraman who is filming and knocks the camera from his hand as Francis catches up with Chris. Chris takes the flashlight from Francis and dives into the lake, shapeshifting into his Bigfoot form midair. The gathered crowd gasps. The cameraman bends down but reaches his camera too late. When he stands up, Bigfoot Chris has already submerged.

"That," Bob says.

"Oh, my," Tom says as the reporters and their cameramen run toward the tunnel.

Underwater with the flashlight in hand, Bigfoot Chris enters the old tunnel and swims until he comes to the connecting shaft. He enters it, follows the light to the end, puts the flashlight in his mouth, and struggles to open the hatch. With great effort and nearly out of breath, Bigfoot Chris is finally able to move the hatch and push it open. He enters the new tunnel. He surfaces, gasping for air. The new bore is dark except for the light from his flashlight.

"Amanda!" he shouts and moves the light until it falls on the overturned canoe.

"Chris, here I am!" Amanda shouts. She has recognized Chris's voice but wonders where he came from and how he got there. But it's him, and she's glad.

"Let's get you out of here." Bigfoot Chris shines the flashlight on Amanda, who is holding on to the overturned canoe. He hands her the flashlight and drops below the surface. Seconds later, he resurfaces into Amanda's circle of light and is illuminated as he was so many years ago by the flashes from Jack's camera. This is what Jack has been telling her. Amanda now remembers that this is the second time she has seen Chris in this form. Jack has been right all along. Chris really is Bigfoot.

Bigfoot Chris steps from the water and lingers a moment, looking at Amanda. Now she knows who he really is, and he knows that she knows. But her safety is all that matters, and he starts to dig. The mixture of muddy rock debris blocking the entrance moves quickly under his strong hands and arms. There is sunlight visible at the top of the blocked portion of the tunnel, and at this pace, with the water receding, it won't take him long to dig them out. He looks again at Amanda and her circle of light and concentrates on her and nothing else. He doubles his efforts and continues to dig toward safety.

The lake level has steadily dropped, and the mouth of the new tunnel is all but dry. In his human form, a muddy Chris emerges with Amanda in his arms. The media flocks to them, and he puts her down.

"How did you get out?" a female reporter asks Amanda.

"Did Bigfoot save you?" a male reporter asks.

Tom and Cleo lead Amanda toward his pickup.

"Leave her alone," Tom says.

"Who was that man carrying you?" the male reporter asks Amanda.

"Is he Bigfoot?" the female reporter asks and turns to Chris. "What is your name, sir?"

"Chris Rainwater."

"Chris," the male reporter says, "are you Bigfoot?"

Chris and Amanda share a look as she gets into Tom's pickup. Tom and Cleo drive her away.

The media rush to surround Chris. Bob Big Sky steps forward. He takes Chris by the arm and leads him through the aggressive crowd. They get into Bob's official Good Bear Lake sheriff's SUV and drive onto the lakeshore road, heading for town. They are followed by media vehicles. Bob drops into four-wheel drive, leaves the road, and heads into the woods. The first media car tries to follow but quickly finds itself stuck in the mud from yesterday's rain. The rest of the caravan piles up behind the first car, as the sheriff's mountain-ready vehicle proceeds to town via a local's shortcut.

"Where are we going?" Chris asks as they drive under the Bigfoot Festival banner on Elk. They pass Gus's office, and Tom's, and Becky's. They continue past the Corner Cupboard, the doctor's office, Ranger Hall, and the big wooden Bigfoot with the welcoming arms.

Bob pulls into his reserved parking place behind city hall. “I’m taking you someplace they can’t get at you.”

“To jail?”

“Un-huh.”

“Gabriel’s idea?” Chris asks, and Bob nods his head, yes.

Chapter 35

A Dog Older Than Me

Newday Marina, Sunday

Jack disembarks his canoe, wades across the deck, and is met by Lulu at the door. He holds up his camera and his bow.

"I've got him now!"

"Jack," Lulu replies.

"I only wish I'd had these photos before last night happened."

"Jack. Last night didn't happen."

"You mean you two didn't ...?"

"No. We didn't."

Jack hugs her. "But, Lulu, that's wonderful, and what's more, I've not only flushed Bigfoot out of hiding but I've also slowed him down."

"What do you mean by that?"

"I shot him with my bow."

"Is he hurt badly?"

"Just a shoulder wound. I passed up an easy kill shot."

"Why?"

"I felt a hand on my shoulder, and I altered my aim. When I turned to see who had touched me, there was no one. I was alone. I had missed on purpose. And I'm not sure why. Or what I'll do if I get a second chance."

"What do you plan for the special session of the town council tomorrow morning?"

Jack holds up his camera. "To use these pictures to prove to everyone I've been right about Chris all along."

"Promise me something first. Before you say anything to anyone, meet me in the hallway outside the meeting room five minutes before the meeting starts."

"Okay, but right now I need to make some hard copies of the evidence." Jack holds up his camera. "I've got him right where I want him. And it's not just a him. It's a them. Lulu, if you can believe it, there's more than one," he adds.

"I can, and I do," she says but doesn't explain.

"Francis is a Bigfoot too. I should have known there was something odd about a dog older than me."

Jack charges off the deck, leaving Lulu shaking her head.

Chapter 36

Innocent Until Proven Guilty

Good Bear Lake Town Hall, Monday

Sheriff Bob has put Chris in jail for his own protection. Outside the town hall, a large crowd has gathered. Several people are looking at the front page of the local paper. The lead story headline reads, *Bigfoot Unmasked!*

Across Elk Avenue, at the Corner Cupboard, Ruthie looks through the front window at the town square as she refills coffee cups, while Lyle reads from the special edition of the newspaper to his customers through the serving window.

"Get this. After saving the life of Amanda James, age thirty-one, local doctor, Chris Rainwater, age thirty-two, is being held in the Good Bear Lake jail by Sheriff Bob Big Sky for questioning by the U.S. Fish and Wildlife Service." Lyle stops to flip a flapjack. "Man, who would have thought?"

"Thought what? That Chris was our friend and now he's not?" Ruthie says.

"Chicken. Nobody like Chris better than me, but if he's an animal—"

"Lyle Firth! You're the one with the four little boys, not Chris."

At the small table in the front window, Becky reads out loud from the paper. "Listen to this. Jack Newday, local volunteer fire captain, age thirty-two, promises a blockbuster announcement at the special session of the town council on Monday."

Ruthie points through the window at the city hall. "The sheriff is coming out now."

On the front steps of city hall, Sheriff Big Sky meets with the media.

"Sheriff. How is Bigfoot doing?" the female reporter asks.

"Can we see him now?" the male reporter interjects before the female reporter can finish.

"All right, folks, one at a time."

"Is Dr. Rainwater Bigfoot?" the male reporter adds.

"Here in our town, a man is still innocent until proven guilty."

"But is Dr. Rainwater really a man?" the female reporter asks.

The crowd begins to chant: "We want Bigfoot! We want Bigfoot!"

Inside the jail, Chris and Francis are playing checkers on the cot in Chris's cell. Francis moves his black piece with his paw, while Shoo and Chip watch the game from between the bars of the cell window above.

"We want Bigfoot!" the crowd outside continues to shout.

Chris makes a move, and Francis takes Chris's remaining red checker. Game over.

"Sorry, Francis. My heart's just not in it today." Chris looks up at Shoo. "Shoo, fly home and check on Gabriel."

Shoo opens his wings. As he does, he knocks Chip out the window but dives and catches the chipmunk before he reaches the ground. He airlifts Chip to the hardware store and hovers outside the mail slot until the earth-bound chipmunk can slip through. Sam cracks open the door and puts a piece of Clara's banana nut bread on the front step. Shoo sees Clara watching him through the window. He eats her somewhat dry banana bread, swallows with some effort, pats his stomach with his wing, and makes a jaybird yummy sound. Better than nothing, always, and he'd hate to hurt Clara's feelings. He waves his thanks to the sweet-faced Clara, who waves back, and in a flash, he rises into the wind and is gone.

At the Blue Moon Inn, the yard is strewn with debris from the flood. Even the old sign, which had been propped against the porch, is nowhere in sight. Amanda comes down the porch steps with her suitcase in hand as Cleo approaches her car from the marina.

"Running away isn't the answer," Cleo says.

"Why not? It worked for my father when he left my mother and me."

"He was wrong. You know how his leaving hurt you both. He chose ambition over the happiness of the two people he loved the most."

"At least we were people!"

"And based on that, you've chosen to leave?"

"What good would it do to stay? No matter what Chris is, or isn't, he's already married to Lulu."

"You're assuming you know more than you do."

Amanda opens her car door and tosses the suitcase in. "What else is there to know?"

"That's the same thing I said over thirty years ago, faced with almost the same situation. And the answer is quite a lot."

"What do you suggest I do?"

Cleo points to the island. "Do what I did. Go see him."

"By him, you mean Gabriel?"

"Hang on. I'll get the boat and run you over."

Chapter 37

Worldwide Bigfoot Pun

Rainwater Island, Monday

Cleo ferries Amanda to the island in her powerboat. Standing on the Rainwater dock, she says to the younger woman, "There he is."

They look to the house and see Gabriel at his bedroom window, waving. Both women wave back. Shoo lands on Gabriel's arm. Gabriel signals them to come up. Shoo squawks loudly and beckons them up with his wing.

"Chris's grandfather has all the answers, then?" Amanda asks.

They start up the steps together.

"Not all, no, but he's the head man around here, and he can help you to understand about Chris."

"Head of what?"

"I'll let him take it from there, and I promise you'll be surprised by what he tells you. Open your mind, as I finally decided to do many years ago. The world we live in contains more wonderful things than we know of, Amanda, and Gabriel Rainwater is one of those things. You'll not meet his like again." Cleo turns and starts back down the steps toward the dock.

"You're not coming with me?"

"No. This is for you to do alone," Cleo says over her shoulder.

At the window above, the jaybird flaps his wings and squawks loudly.

"And don't worry about that noisy ball of feathers. His name is Shoo, and he can be a tad loud and a bit tedious, but down deep inside he's a real sweetie."

As Cleo returns to the dock, Amanda looks up at Gabriel. He appears to be saying something to the big bird, who then quiets down and flies over the steps and hovers above her as if to lead her up. Amanda remembers the fir tree and the limb-hopping wooden owl in the barn as she follows the black bird, who apparently understands English. This entire island, like the barn, is not run-of-the-mill, but she still wonders what Gabriel can possibly tell her to change the fact that Jack was right. Chris is Bigfoot.

"Chris isn't human," she shouts up at Shoo, "and that's that."

Shoo flies to Gabriel, lands on his outstretched arm, and repeats in jaybird what Amanda has just said about Chris, concluding with a squawked, "And that's that."

Gabriel shakes his head and says to Shoo, "We'll just have to see then, won't we?" He shouts down to Amanda. "Come in. We're up in my room."

Amanda passes through the great room with the big stone fireplace and climbs the stairs that lead to the second floor. She finds Gabriel still at the window in his bedroom. He and the jaybird are looking out at the now placid lake.

"When the wind is still like today, the water looks so blue. Do you like blue?" Gabriel asks.

"It's my favorite color."

"Mine, too."

Shoo hops from Gabriel's arm onto Amanda's shoulder.

"Hello, Shoo," Amanda says, eye to eye with the jaybird. "Cleo said that was your name. Is that right?"

Shoo smiles a tight-lipped smile and squawks again—a definite jaybird yes.

"Cleo is always so nice to Shoo, even though she hardly speaks a word of his language," Gabriel says. "You don't happen to speak jaybird, do you?"

Amanda shakes her head. "Not a word."

"No, I wouldn't think so, too high pitched for human ears."

"But not for yours?"

"No, not for mine."

Amanda overflows with questions. "Why am I here?"

"My doing. I asked Cleo to run you over. When you were small, you were the closest thing I had to a granddaughter. I felt I owed it to you to help you understand about Chris."

Shoo hops onto the small table by the window as Gabriel waves goodbye to Cleo below. The sound of Cleo's boat leaving the dock follows immediately.

"Is Cleo leaving?" Amanda says.

"She is."

"How will I get back to the inn?"

"Can you still paddle a canoe?"

"I'm not sure. It's been such a long time."

"It's like riding a bike. Hard to forget."

Shoo squawks.

"She heard me, Shoo. No need to repeat. Besides, we've already determined that Amanda doesn't understand what you're saying."

Shoo frowns and shuts up. More's the pity.

Gabriel takes a seat at the table and motions toward the chair next to his. "Have a seat and fire away."

Shoo sits on the tabletop, drops his skinny legs over the side, crosses his ankles, and kicks his big bird feet in the air.

Amanda takes the chair beside Gabriel. "Twice now Chris has risked everything to save my life. Once on the lake when we were kids and then again yesterday at the tunnel. Why would he do that?"

"Because he loves you, Amanda."

Shoo squawks in jaybird. "*Because he loves you, Amanda.*"

"I've got this, Shoo," Gabriel says. "Why don't you fly to town and see how the council meeting is coming along?"

Shoo opens his broad wings and whisks out the open window.

Gabriel returns to Amanda. "You were about to say?"

"But Chris isn't human. How can he love me?"

"You're right, he isn't, but you're thinking love is exclusively a human emotion. Not true. But then, you don't really believe in love, do you?"

"No, not for a long time, not since my parents divorced and my mother died. Even if I did, wouldn't both parties in a relationship still have to be human?"

"Actually, that's not an insurmountable problem. We have a provision to get around that little glitch," Gabriel replies and shows Amanda his right hand. "Remind me later to tell you how the hand thing works."

"You just said we."

"We, because Chris isn't alone." Gabriel picks up a photo from the table and hands it to her. It's a picture of Gabriel, Chris, Francis, and Shoo. "Take, for example, the other three you see in this photograph with Chris."

"But Frank is a dog."

"Yes, in the same way that Chris is human and Who outside in the barn is an owl. And this Frank business of his is just a passing fad. He's really the same old Francis you and Chris knew when you were kids."

Gabriel explains that Francis was originally from the

Cotswold District in England before he immigrated to the US and came to live with them many years ago. It was his idea to plant the spruce trees in a circle around the big wooden sculpture downtown. He said it reminded him of his childhood home.

"And Shoo?"

"Oh, we couldn't do without Shoo. He acts as our eyes in the sky. He's originally from Australia, but he loves the mountains and transferred from the outback here to us more than fifty years ago."

Amanda points to Gabriel's image. "Cleo said you were the head guy. Is this what she meant?"

"I'm afraid so. I'm the boss Bigfoot in this part of Colorado. We prefer the name ranger, even though the more popular name does provide us with a cover that fits our mission. And I will admit, by human standards, we do have rather large feet when we're in our natural form, which allows us to run and swim faster than you all. We also have other features not shared by humans or animals. We live a much longer time. I've been head ranger for 150 years and was 175 on my last birthday. And, in all modesty, we're unusually intelligent, have great strength, and our fur keeps us warm in all weathers."

"You said in your natural form?"

"We have the power to shapeshift, to change our forms. Chris and I prefer human. Francis likes dog and Shoo, jaybird. As the head ranger in this district, I can change into pretty much whatever I want whenever I want. Most of the time, I'm happy to be what you see here before you, a retired old wood-carving doctor, but sometimes I find it necessary to become something other. I do an especially good skunk."

Amanda decides to suspend her disbelief, takes a deep breath, and asks, "Was that you under the porch on Saturday with Cleo?"

"It was, yes, but a skunk is harder to do than you might think. Getting the smell just right is the hard part. I finally nailed it the night Chris and Lulu got married."

"You stunk up their wedding night then?"

"Ruined it totally. Mostly it was my doing, but Francis and Shoo did help. But after we cut the water heater back on and they washed off the stink, they forgave us and spent the rest of the night by the fire, wrapped in blankets, playing checkers. I think they were relieved by what we had done. You see, Chris and Lulu really don't love each other."

Amanda and Gabriel trade smiles. Cleo was right. Everything Gabriel is telling her, in his matter-of-fact way, is surprising her. Nothing he has said so far fits with her notion of reality, but as Cleo suggested, maybe Amanda's reality isn't the only one.

She looks again at the picture and then returns it to Gabriel. "You mentioned your mission. What would that be?"

Gabriel replaces the photo on the tabletop. "There are many others like the four of us scattered throughout the world. Each works to serve a similar place, a place that functions as a spiritual conduit for human spirits coming into and going out of this life."

He explains that these places are known as portals and are watched over by similar uniquely qualified members of the Federated Union of Rangers, or FUR. He smiles again. "The name FUR is somewhat of an inside joke and a bit of a worldwide Bigfoot pun I'm afraid."

He adds that at Good Bear Lake, the portal is located here on the island inside their barn and that protecting the portal is the reason the Rainwater family lives here. He reminds her of the blue light on the lake the night her mother died.

"It was the same light you saw on Friday night at the rehearsal, when Ruthie's baby was born. The blue light means the portal is open and love, the color of which is blue, our favorite color, is being released into the world, as it was on the night your mother left us."

"Is Lulu a member of your union?"

"She is, as is her father, Bob Big Sky. Chris feels that he needs to marry Lulu, the daughter of the president of our board of directors, because he believes he is next in line to fill my Rainwater shoes, so to speak, as head of our ranger federation. Love matters to us, however, as much as it does to you humans."

"And so, you stopped their honeymoon?"

"Actually, we didn't have to. Better, warm, and good did that for us. Another inside joke, I'm afraid." He gets up and returns to the window. "Okay, now it's your turn again."

"Why are you telling me this? Wouldn't it have been easier just to let me go?"

"Yes, but that would have hurt Chris and you both. I love each of you very much and want you to be happy."

Amanda stands, goes over to the armoire, and opens the door. "I wondered where that odor was coming from. Is this why you always smell like piñon pine?"

"An occupational hazard. That smell permeates every stitch of my clothes. They pick it up from the portal downstairs in the barn."

"The barn with the fir tree that grows indoors and the wooden owl named Who, who jumps from limb to limb, and the English Labrador who likes to be called Frank and the jaybird named Shoo who understands English and the 175-year-old man who wears clothes that smell like piñon pine and can change into a skunk when it suits him and has a Bigfoot grandson named Chris, all of whom work to protect a spiritual channel known as the portal. Is that what you're asking me to believe?"

"It is, but you have to remember, believing is always the hard part."

She reaches inside the armoire, touches Chris's Bigfoot festival costume, and looks at Gabriel, who then says, "That Chris isn't human is true. Is that still just that then?"

"You heard me talking?"

"Not me, Shoo. Our eyes in the sky also has big ears."

Cleo had been right about Gabriel. Amanda will not likely see his like again. "No. That is no longer just that."

"Any more questions?"

Like Cleo, Amanda has made her decision. "Only one." She removes the Bigfoot costume headpiece from the armoire. "What can I do to help?"

"I'll ask you again. Can you still paddle a canoe?"

She puts on the headpiece, and she answers in a muffled voice. "Definitely."

Chapter 38

Can't Be in Two Places at One Time

Town dock, Good Bear Lake, Monday

The female reporter speaks on camera: "So we say goodbye to Good Bear Lake, the location of the most intriguing human, or should I say Bigfoot, interest story that this reporter has seen in many a moon. Bigfoot, the legendary creature whose existence, despite what we've seen and heard over the last two days, has yet to be documented."

Bigfoot paddling in a canoe out on the lake suddenly appears in her cameraman's viewfinder. He leaves the reporter and follows Bigfoot with his lens as the canoe moves away.

At town hall, Jack races up the stairs, waving a fistful of photo prints at Lulu, who is waiting for him, as agreed, in the hallway outside the council meeting room. This morning is to be his long-awaited vindication.

"I've got Chris now, Lulu. And these photographs will prove it."

"Are you sure this is what you want?"

"Sure, I'm sure. Why wouldn't I be?"

"Well. . . ."

Jack shows Lulu his photos of Bigfoot Chris trying to turn the spillway wheel alone and failing and then of Bigfoot Chris and Bigfoot Francis working together and getting it done.

"Aren't these amazing?"

"Amazing but not unexpected," Lulu says softly.

"What was that?" Jack asks.

"Gabriel said it would be a two Bigfoot job, and he was right, as usual."

Jack is confused. "Gabriel said what?"

Lulu shakes her head, pushes Jack into the small hall coat closet, and closes the door. The small space is lightless.

"Before you show these pictures to anyone else, you might want to consider this. Do you remember how Chris became Bigfoot?"

"How can I forget?"

"Did it go something like this?" Lulu suddenly grows as she changes into her own beautiful brown-eyed, brown-skinned Bigfoot form, filling the dark closet. As gorgeous a Bigfoot girl as ever there was.

Jack is pushed backward into the coat rack, his eyes wide. "Pretty much."

Lulu exits the closet in human form. A dazed Jack follows her into the hall. Sam and Clara Summertime walk by. They both wave at Jack, as does Chip from inside Sam's shirt pocket. Bumfuzzled, Jack appears fine with seeing a chipmunk waving at him from a shirt pocket, and he waves back.

"That chipmunk doesn't happen to be a Bigfoot too, perchance, does he?"

Lulu smiles at Jack. "Well, we prefer the term ranger, but yes. In fact, all three of them are."

"Sam and Clara Summertime? At the hardware store where I've been shopping all my life? The man who keeps our powerboat running and the lady who carries hammers in her purse and makes us that crusty old banana nut bread every Christmas?"

"The very same. Sam, Clara, and Chip are a threesome and among our finest."

"Our finest? Are there more of you?"

"Oh my, yes," Lulu replies and leads a glassy-eyed Jack into the jam-packed meeting room.

She deposits him in his usual seat in the front row. Jack looks around the overfilled chamber, squints at the people seated on either side of him, and then studies the members of the council, who are sitting in their usual places at the front table. On one side of the table, Becky, Tom, and Gus are busy looking at their notes with their heads down. Lulu passes by these three and shakes her head, no, at Jack. She moves to the other side to Rev. Dinky and her father, Sheriff Bob, and whispers in their ears. Both men smile and wave at Jack. Dinky makes a big gesture with his arms, throwing them over his head as if he were exploding upward. Then he laughs.

"Dinky too," Jack says aloud to the man sitting beside him.

"Dinky, too, what?" the man replies.

"Never mind."

Sheriff Bob gavels the meeting to order. What, Jack thinks, could he say about any of this that wouldn't implicate Lulu? As he watches Lulu take her seat, he realizes that, whatever she is, he still loves her.

"Okay, people. Gabriel has asked me to help out this morning, seeing as how Chris is who he is and all," Sheriff Bob says.

Shoo flies in through the window and lands on Gus's shoulder.

Tom Throttle takes Becky's hand, and they both stand. "Before we start, I, that is Becky and I, would like to go on record as supporting Chris 110 percent. Whoever, or whatever, he is, he's still our friend." Tom gives Becky's hand a squeeze.

Bob responds, “Thank you, Tom and Becky. The chair recognizes Jack Newday.”

Jack looks at Bob with a blank face. Bob is his fellow firefighter at the firehouse, and the town sheriff, and a Bigfoot. “And Dinky, and both Summertimes, and their pocket-sized chipmunk friend,” he says aloud.

“Did you say something Jack?” Bob asks.

Jack mumbles to himself. “Who’s next?”

“Would you mind repeating that?” Bob replies.

“No, thank you, I’m good,” Jack adds and falls quiet.

Suddenly the female reporter and her cameraman rush in and interrupt the meeting. “He’s headed for the island!” they shout.

“Who’s headed for the island?” the male reporter asks.

The cameraman plays the video on his hand-held screen. People crowd around.

“Bigfoot is out on the lake, paddling a canoe, and he’s heading for the island,” the male reporter says, and the room immediately begins to clear.

Tom has a question: “How can Chris be Bigfoot if he’s here in jail, and Bigfoot is out on the lake in a canoe?”

“He can’t be in two places at one time, can he?” Becky says.

Jack sits quietly, making a paddling motion. You wouldn’t think so. But Jack is no longer so sure. Of anything much. Lulu looks at him and smiles.

“What do you say, Gus?” Sheriff Bob asks.

Shoo looks Gus in the eye. This time, he doesn’t flinch. “It may mean my job, but yes, I agree with Becky,” Gus says.

Shoo squawks at him in jaybird, "*Good on you, mate.*"

Sheriff Bob looks at the still silent Jack. "Jack, do you have anything to add?"

Clearly poor Jack has run up the white flag. He shakes his head. He has nothing to say, again. He holds up his envelope filled with incriminating photos. Shoo grabs them in his beak.

"You, too, bird?" he says to Shoo.

Shoo nods a yes, me, too. He drops the photos into a nearby trash can and then squawks out another, "*Good on you,*" in jaybird.

Sheriff Bob stands. "Then this council, by virtue of the 'you can't be in two places at one time rule,' declares Chris Rainwater not to be Bigfoot and hereby authorizes the sheriff, namely me, to release Chris and his dog, Francis, immediately." Sheriff Bob sounds his gavel. "Meeting adjourned."

The room is now empty except for Cleo and Jack.

"Mother, you know the coat closet in the hall outside?"

"Yes, dear?"

"I was in it just before the meeting with Lulu."

"Yes, dear. I understand. You're both grown-ups."

Especially Lulu, as Jack now knows. They walk into the hall, arm in arm. "But, Mother, Lulu's not who I thought she was."

"Yes, dear. Few of us ever are."

Jack glances at the closet as they pass. If Lulu is a Bigfoot, how can he love her? But he does. "But I still love her. How can that be?"

"Maybe because you're not who you think you are either."

"What does that mean?"

"I'll be able to tell you soon."

"When?"

"Won't be long now. When Gabriel...."

"When Gabriel what?" Jack follows his mother down the stairs toward the front door.

Cleo holds the door open for her confused son. "Can't tell you yet."

As Cleo and Jack exit the building, Bob Big Sky escorts Chris and Francis out the front door and down the front steps.

"It couldn't have been Gabriel. He's much too sick to paddle a canoe," Chris says to Bob.

"Who then? Everybody else was at the meeting."

"I'd better get home and find out."

As they leave city hall, Chris and Jack glance at each other but don't speak. Chris and Francis then hustle toward town dock. Jack and Cleo head for the marina.

At the marina, the yard is filled with media people. Jack and Cleo arrive as reporters and their cameramen in life jackets leave the dock in borrowed rowboats and canoes.

"What's all the excitement about?" Cleo asks the female reporter.

"Bigfoot's headed for the island."

"I need to warn Gabriel," Cleo says to Jack.

Jack runs to his pickup. "I don't understand any of this, but Chris is out again. I'm still not sure about him. I'm going with you."

"Chris poses no danger to you or anyone else," Cleo says. "Just the opposite."

"I have to see that for myself," Jack replies and retrieves his bow and quiver and runs for their powerboat.

At the town dock, Chris sees Cleo and Jack move off in their motorized craft. He changes into his Bigfoot form and tells Francis to follow and to meet him at home later. He dives into the lake and swims at top speed for the island.

Out on the lake, Cleo and Jack bump over the water,

quickly overtake the media boats, and pass them. Cleo eyes Jack's bow and quiver.

"You won't need those. Remember what you said about Lulu," Cleo says.

"Chris isn't Lulu," Jack replies.

Bigfoot Chris also catches the media flotilla. Seeing him coming, the first cameramen stands to film. Bigfoot Chris rocks his boat and causes the cameramen and his camera to hit the water. He swims on to the next boat and does the same. Cameraman and camera number two go into the drink. Bigfoot Chris repeats the process until all the cameramen and all the cameras are wet.

The male reporter helps his cameraman back aboard their boat. "Did you get the shot?"

The cameraman empties water out of his camera. "Are you kidding?"

Chapter 39

The Hand Thing

Rainwater Island, Monday

Cleo and Jack step off their boat at the dock and look out at the fleet of rowboats coming their way.

"Somebody has to head off those reporters," Cleo says.

"Stay here if you want, but I'm going up," Jack replies. He starts onto the steps with his bow and quiver.

"Jack, wait for me, please."

Jack isn't sure what he will find above. In fact, he's not sure about much of what he has just seen or heard—especially what he has learned about Lulu—except that he still loves her. Then there is Chris, whom he has thought of as his enemy for most of his life. Where does Chris fit into this confusing picture? Is he the risk to the community that Jack has always thought? Before Lulu's confession, he had been clear on everything. After it, very little. And now, nothing.

At the top of the steps, Jack approaches the barn with reticence and then enters the darkened space. He passes through the inanimate forest of wooden animals, under the limbs of the living Douglas fir. He hesitates at the door that leads down to the portal. He puts his hand on the knob, opens the door, but then doesn't enter.

Who animates, moves lower in the tree, and lowers his head into what passes for a great-horned-owl bow. He holds out his wing, and points ahead, indicating that Jack may pass.

Jack nods at the big bird and moves on to Gabriel's workshop. Inside, he picks up the sign Gabriel has been working on. The still incomplete name plate now reads: *Blue Moon In.*

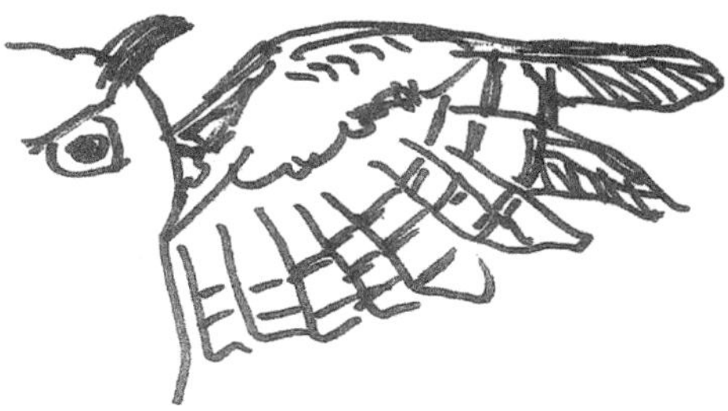

He then hears a noise in the barn, puts down the sign, and goes back inside.

At Rainwater dock, Bigfoot Chris comes out of the water and shapeshifts into his human form. The media boats are closing in. He joins Cleo at the stairs to the house. "Where's Jack?"

Cleo points up the steps. "He's gone to the barn, and he has his bow with him."

Chis rubs his right shoulder. "Head off those reporters," he says and charges up the steps.

The reporters arrive and pour onto the dock. Cleo holds up her hands, stops the rush, and points toward the beach. "Hey, everybody. He went that way." The media crowd hurries off in the wrong direction.

Inside the barn, Jack makes his way through the shadows. Bow in hand, he sees a large form standing among the wooden animals. He loads an arrow. Even in the dark, it's clear to him that this must be Bigfoot Chris, his long-time nemesis. He raises his bow as the staircase to the basement suddenly fills with blue light. Jack feels a presence at his shoulder, the same presence he felt in his canoe at the spillway. The light changes from a diffuse blue haze into a well-formed outline of a man, who now stands beside him.

Chris, in his human form, arrives at the door to the barn,

and the apparition fades. A second Bigfoot appears and shields the first with its body. The first Bigfoot removes its headpiece. It's Amanda, wearing Chris's Bigfoot costume. She was the one the cameraman had seen and filmed earlier paddling the canoe on the lake.

"Jack, it's Amanda," Chris shouts as the second shielding Bigfoot changes into Gabriel.

Jack lowers his bow and withdraws the arrow.

Gabriel speaks to Amanda: "Wait outside for Cleo, Amanda. I need to speak with Chris and Jack alone." She leaves by the back door.

"Who was that we just saw with Jack?" Chris asks Gabriel.

"William," Gabriel says.

"My Uncle William?" Chris replies.

"Yes."

"Who's William?" Jack asks. He has no idea what just happened or who Gabriel and Chris are talking about.

"There are a number of things you don't know about yourself, Jack. And some that not even Chris knows. One of them is the rest of William's story."

Gabriel tells Jack and Chris how his oldest boy, William, fell in love with a Good Bear Lake woman and decided to convert to human so they could marry and how the couple had lived as man and wife in town and had a son. "The couple's name was Newday, the man was Bill, short for William, and the woman, Cleo. Their son's name was Jack," Gabriel adds.

"Chris's Uncle William was married to my mother?" Jack says.

"Yes, Jack. William, my oldest boy, was your father," Gabriel continues. "After William died in the avalanche with John, William's younger brother, I decided that neither Jack nor Chris should know who the other was, since they would be living in different worlds, until the time was right. And that time has finally come," Gabriel concludes.

"But the man I saw was real, and my father is gone," Jack says.

"Real, yes, but not in the earthly sense. William is a spiritual being now, part of the continuum between life and death that moves freely through our portal, protected and watched over by our family, by your family, Jack."

Gabriel hugs Jack, and they hold the embrace. "Welcome home," he says to Jack, "Grandson." Gabriel motions to Chris to join them.

Chris steps forward and joins in the embrace. "Welcome, cousin," he says.

"Sorry about the shoulder, Chris. And for the way I've acted toward you since we were kids."

"I was no better to you," Chris says. "How about we start over from here?"

As crazy as it sounds, it's all beginning to make sense to Jack. It explains many things, including his warm feelings for Gabriel and for the island. He smiles at Chris. "I can do that."

Chris rubs his right shoulder. "And thank you for not shooting any straighter at the dam."

Jack now knows that it was his father at the spillway. "You can thank my father for that."

"I will. The next time I see him."

Cleo and Amanda come in together. Gabriel tells Cleo that he has just told Jack much of his story. It's the reason why when Jack passed the tree, Who, the portal's great-horned guardian, knew immediately who he was and allowed him to enter.

"William was always one of Who's favorites," Cleo says to Jack.

"You have my permission now, Cleo, to tell Jack the rest. As my older son's boy, he'll have a big decision to make," Gabriel says and then turns to Amanda. "Do me a favor, Amanda. Promise not to leave town until you and Chris have had a chance to sit down and talk."

"I promise," Amanda replies, looking now at Chris. "I'll be at the inn."

"I'll be over in a bit," Chris says.

Gabriel coughs. "He won't be long."

In the powerboat headed toward town, Amanda sits aft by herself, thinking, while Jack and Cleo are forward. This time Jack drives the boat. As Cleo completes the story of how she and his father got together, Jack pulls up to the marina.

"Anyway, that was how Bill converted," Cleo finishes.

Jack hops out and ties off the boat. "The hand thing?"

"The hand thing. Then Gabriel altered Bill's appearance so as not to confuse the people in town, and he gave us the name, Newday. Head Rangers can do stuff like that, you know."

"I do now." Jack tosses his bow and quiver into the lake and starts across the dock. There is only one thing on his mind, one question left to be answered, and he needs to find Lulu to get that answer.

"Where are you going, son?" Cleo says.

"To find Lulu."

"Look for her at the hall."

"Thanks, mom."

Chapter 40

Name to Be Proud Of

Good Bear Lake, Monday

At the town dock, the annual festival fireworks display is ready to go. Dinky is head of the crew, as usual, and he studies the sky. Dark. It's time. He lights the first fuse. The rocket ignites and climbs into the night, trailing fire.

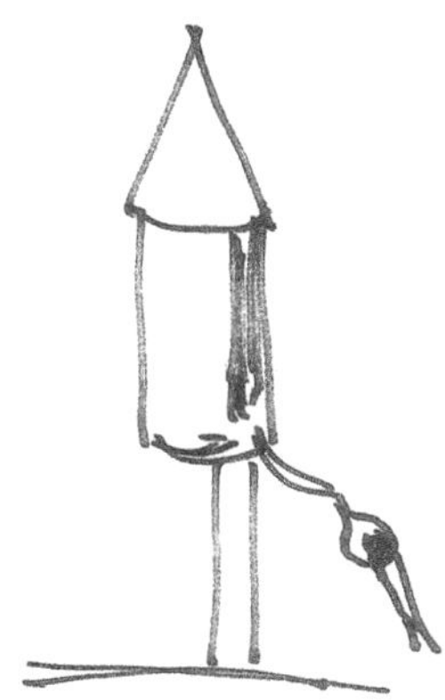

Multicolored flame trails burst over the water, as the rocket explodes. Dinky has begun the highlight of the Bigfoot Days celebration.

Upstairs in Gabriel's bedroom on Rainwater Island, Chris stands at the window, looking out at the lake. "Dinky has started his fireworks show." He watches a second rocket explode over the lake and hears Gabriel struggling to catch his breath. "Grandfather!"

"Chris. Take me to the barn."

Chris lifts Gabriel from his bed and carries him to the stairs, followed by Francis and Shoo. When they reach the great room downstairs, Gabriel asks to be put down. Chris sets him on his feet, and his grandfather looks around the familiar room. He puts his hands on the ancient stone fireplace as if he were saying goodbye to an old friend.

"I'm ready now, Chris," Gabriel says, indicating the door.

They cross the yard arm in arm, Gabriel leaning on Chris. They enter the barn. Once inside, they make their way past the inanimate animals and the tree with its wooden birds on high limbs and into the woodworking shop. Gabriel puts on his multicolored coat and sits at his workbench in front of the new sign. Selecting a chisel and picking up his mallet, he completes the second *n* of the last word of the name that is now fully carved into the sign's name plate: *Blue Moon Inn.*

"Chris, when you visit Amanda, take her this gift. And tell her I love her."

"I will, Grandfather."

Booms from Dinky's fireworks continue. Francis, with Shoo riding on his back, enters the workshop. Gabriel signals Francis to his side. He puts his hand on the big dog's head. "Francis was my father's name. Like you, my old friend, he was steadfast and loyal. Francis is a name to be proud of, so no more of this Frank business, okay?"

Francis nods his agreement. Gabriel then removes the leather band from his right wrist, leans forward, and slips it around the black bird's neck. "My faithful Shoo, when you see the signal, and it won't be hard to recognize, take this to the hall and give it to Jack." He strokes the creature's feathered head.

Shoo looks sadly at Gabriel as Francis drops his head. And then, Shoo flies out the open window with the symbol of the head ranger's office around his long neck.

"Chris, take me to the portal," Gabriel says and walks slowly with his grandson through the barn. As he passes, each of the wooden animals animates at Gabriel's soft touch. The three big birds, Red, Honk, and Who, flutter to the lowest limb of the great tree and perch side by side. They lower their heads as Gabriel approaches so that they might receive his final blessing.

"Wait here with the others," Gabriel says to Francis.

The big dog crouches by the door to the staircase and begins to cry.

Gabriel pats his big back. "Don't be sad, my old English friend. We'll miss each other, but we'll both be fine. And I'll come for you when it's your time."

Francis sniffs and manages a smile as Gabriel and Chris go on together. At the bottom of the stairs, the portal door opens as if it recognizes Gabriel, even without his wristband.

"Come in with me," Gabriel says to Chris.

"Am I allowed?"

"This one time, yes."

They enter. The room is reminiscent of the meeting room at the hall, devoid of furniture. Like the hall, the stark white walls stretch up and up, only this room has no visible ceiling and the air inside is distinctly blue. Piñon pine needles cover the rough-hewn oak floors. The Cocker Spaniel puppy asleep in the basket in the far corner stirs, opens his eyes, tumbles from his cushion, and wobbles to Gabriel on fat feet.

Chris is unsure of what to expect. "What do we do now?"

"Now we wait for them," Gabriel says. He picks up the party-colored puppy, pets him, and gets a lick on his hand in return.

"For whom?"

At the far end of the large room is a doorway that has no door. The color of the air on the other side is an even deeper blue, the endless blue of a cloudless Rocky Mountain sky in summertime. Two men enter through the open doorway, haloed by a breathtaking bluer than blue that follows from inside.

"My two spirit guides," Gabriel says.

The first man, Chris recognizes from earlier as Jack's father, William. The second is Chris's own father, John, Gabriel's youngest son. The two brothers, William and John, embrace Gabriel, enfolding him into their blanket of deep blue. The threesome turns to Chris, all now haloed in blue.

"Thanks, Uncle William, for spoiling Jack's aim," Chris says.

William doesn't speak but smiles a spiritual *you're welcome.*

Gabriel says to Chris, "William is my eldest son, which makes Jack the natural heir to the Rainwater legacy. Jack's destiny, Chris, if he chooses to accept it, is to become head ranger and has always been. Your destiny is whatever you believe is right for you."

"How will I know what's right for me, Grandfather?"

Chris's father, John, moves to hug his son. As they embrace, Gabriel says, "We'll just have to see then, won't we?"

John shakes his ethereal head in agreement with Gabriel's assessment. Each of the brothers then takes his father by an arm.

"Don't worry. I'll be fine," Gabriel says to Chris. "My two boys are with me now."

Chris pulls Gabriel close. "Grandfather, will you come for me when my time comes?"

"I will, as will your mother and father."

John nods. Yes, they'll all be there. Gabriel removes his favorite jacket and gives it to Chris. Chris puts on the old coat.

"I love you, Grandfather."

"And I love you, my grandson."

Chris and Gabriel again embrace. Gabriel grips the sleeve of his cherished coat, now worn by Chris. He lets slowly go of the earthly fabric, once so important to him in life, and follows his two sons to the open doorway. The puppy in his arms licks his face. Gabriel turns, waves goodbye to Chris, and then follows his two sons inside. Suddenly the intense light from the inner room flows like a blue avalanche through the door that leads up to the staircase.

Chris is swept along by the flood of bluer-than-blue, up the stairs, and into the barn. Inside, the animals, including Francis, remain quiet as the enormity of blue fills the barn, blows open the windows and the outside door, and escapes into the night as a torrent of unstoppable love. The head ranger of Good Bear Lake is gone.

Chapter 41

You Were the Man for the Job

Town of Good Bear Lake, Monday

At the boat dock, Dinky halts the fireworks as the expansive blue floods across the water and covers the face of the moon, creating a super blue moon the likes of which has not been seen over Good Bear Lake for 150 years, since the death of Gabriel's father, Francis.

"Wrap it up, boys," Dinky says to the members of his crew. "No way can we compete with this."

Flying just ahead of the flow of blue, Shoo, with Gabriel's leather wristband around his neck, heads for town. He flies in and out of the low-lying clouds, changing directions several times. He isn't seeing well because tears are blurring his vision.

Jack arrives at Ranger Hall and enters the foyer just as the blue light arrives. He has lived in Good Bear Lake his whole life, and this is the first time he's been inside the building. Yet, he feels in his heart he has truly come home. His mother was right. He now understands many things, including his unexplained connection to Gabriel and the island and the reason he has always felt that there was something missing in his life. Because it wasn't his real life. This is.

The door leading to the stairs glows faintly blue and then opens spontaneously. Jack enters and climbs past the portraits of his relatives and past the next to last portrait of Gabriel. The plaque below the painting now documents, *Gabriel Rainwater, 1868–2018.*

He stops for a moment in front of the plaque below the empty frame, which reads, *Jack Newday Rainwater, 2018–*. Jack, taking two steps at a time now, climbs to the rooftop, where he finds the ranger directors waiting for him on the overlook. Lulu is at the front of the gathering. She steps forward to greet him.

At the Corner Cupboard, Tom and Becky hold hands across the window table as the three Firth boys burst in. Instead of chasing, they are now being chased by the no-longer-shy little tourist girl. All four children run out the front door into the blue night, heading for the square, the screen door banging shut behind them.

Arriving in town, Shoo flies low over the city hall lawn and lands on the outstretched arm of Gabriel's Bigfoot wooden statue. The four children from the Corner Cupboard slow down as they pass under the arm and watch the blue electric LED lights on the surrounding spruce trees go out. Like Dinky's fireworks, they are icing on a cake that needs none. Shoo waits for a breeze and then rises into the blue night and moves on.

On Ranger Hall's rooftop, Jack and Lulu stand together beneath the bluest moon the town has experienced since the death of Francis Rainwater. Jack finally knows who he really is, the son of William Rainwater, and that he is the next in a long line of Rainwater head rangers.

"You know who you are now?" Lulu asks.

"I do, yes," Jack replies.

"And who I am?"

"Yes." He not only knows who Lulu is but also why he has always felt that they are meant for each other. Because they are. Mistletoe is no longer required. They kiss lightly.

"And what this blue moon means?"

"Yes. That my grandfather is gone." But Jack has gotten to be with Gabriel before he departed and, for the first time, has been made to feel like he belongs and that this is his destiny.

"What's next for us?" Lulu asks.

Jack holds out his right hand. "For you to take my hand."

Shoo lands on Jack's forearm. Jack removes the leather wristband from the bird's neck and puts it on his own right wrist. Lulu shapeshifts into her beautiful Bigfoot form and takes Jack's hand.

Engulfed in blue, Jack changes into his own unique Bigfoot form. His intense expression has become a mixture of resolve and compassion common to all Rainwater head rangers. One at a time, the directors shapeshift, come forward, and congratulate Jack.

There are big hands out and big smiles on big faces all around. Bigfoot Dinky is followed by Bigfoot Bob, who hugs Bigfoot Lulu as she stands beside Bigfoot Jack.

"Daughter, I always liked Bill and Cleo, and I know I will respect and work well with their son, Jack, the legitimate Rainwater heir."

Bigfoot Jack smiles.

"You and Lulu are the perfect match, lineage-wise," Bigfoot Bob adds.

Bigfoot Sam grabs and pumps Bigfoot Jack's hand furiously.

Bigfoot Clara slows him down. "Take it easy, dear. Jack's going to need that hand for quite a while."

Bigfoot Sam lets go. "Right, sorry, boss," he says to Jack.

"Always knew you were the man for the job, Jack," Bigfoot Chip says. He steps back into a nearby table, stumbles, but recovers without mishap.

"Thank you," Bigfoot Jack replies.

"Chipmunk Who Falls A Lot is my formal name, but please call me Chip."

"Thank you, Chip, for the vote of confidence." Bigfoot Jack looks at Bigfoot Dinky. "What do you think, Dink?"

"No more bow and arrows?"

"Tossed them in the lake. And we can lose those hunting trophies in my office and let that poor bear out front rest in peace."

"How about helping me wax the truck next year for the parade?"

Bigfoot Jack pats Bigfoot Dinky on his broad back. "Nothing I'd rather do."

"No problem, then," Bigfoot Dinky says.

Shoo shapeshifts. "No problem," he says, as Bigfoot Shoo.

The entire group moves to the railing and the rangers look toward the island, which glows like an enormous blue diamond in a liquid blue setting. A new day is about to dawn, and the portent for that day is not just okay. It's warm and good.

In the town square, the three Firth boys and the little tourist girl sit on the lawn below the Bigfoot statue and feel the cool blue grass with their children fingers. They are quiet and still for the first time this week. The wooden Gabriel's kind face above looks down on them with an inscrutable smile.

Across the street, Tom and Becky, still holding hands, sit on the long wooden bench in front of the Corner Cupboard.

They are joined by Lyle and Ruthie and their new baby boy, whom the Firths have decided to call Gabriel.

The four adults look up at the blue moon, now in full bloom. "Best I've ever seen," Becky says.

"The very best," Ruthie agrees and kisses baby Gabriel's forehead.

Tom smiles his agreement, and Lyle says, "Worth every penny.

Chapter 42

Set of Blueberry Checkers

Town of Good Bear Lake, Monday

With the blue moon event concluded, Chris and Francis pull up to the town dock in their canoe. Francis gets out. Chris, wearing Gabriel's multicolored coat, remains in the boat with Gabriel's newly completed Blue Moon Inn sign.

"Congratulate Jack for me, Francis. Tell him I'll see him soon."

Francis nods and lopes off toward town. On his way down Elk, he decides he should do something special in remembrance of Gabriel. Francis thinks as he runs down the street, dodging potholes and crossing the bridge over Coal Creek. He looks at the old carriage house, and he remembers their adventure with the skunk, Gabriel's favorite other self. He determines to add something new to his repertoire in his friend's honor. Clearly there's an opening for a skunk. It'll be tough, but he's up for giving it a go. Besides, he's a natural for the fuzzy and the black parts. The white stripe from his tail to his nose shouldn't be too hard to work out. The holdup will be getting the smell just right. Finding places to practice will not be easy with that bunch of wooden heads in the barn always hanging around. He'll have to keep his eye open for opportunities. But skunk it will be.

Francis goes straight to the hall and into the foyer. He hears Ebay's collar bell tinkle and spots the cat crouched in the corner. He changes into his Bigfoot form, snatches up Ebay, and looks her in the eye. "Why have you been following me?"

Suddenly, Ebay shapeshifts into a sleek Bigfoot girl, every bit as exotic as she was as a cat. "I just had to meet you."

Bigfoot Francis is surprised but pleasantly so. "Me? Why?"

"Checkers are my passion. Your recent article in the *Federation Today* magazine, 'Checkers, the Next Frontier,' blew me away. I am such a fan, Francis." She smiles. "May I call you Francis?"

He remembers Gabriel's admonition. "Please. And do it often."

He suggests she come in with him and allow him to introduce her to the others. He opens the door by putting his Bigfoot hand in the Bigfoot blue box, and they start up the stairs leading to the roof. Passing the portrait of Francis Rainwater, Bigfoot Francis points to name on the plaque below the painting. "Francis. Same as me."

"A name to be proud of," Bigfoot Ebay replies.

Bigfoot Francis smiles. "I've always thought so."

Shoo flies down from the roof and waves with his wing at Bigfoot Francis and Bigfoot Ebay as he passes overhead.

"How are things going up there?" Bigfoot Francis calls up to him. Shoo does a happy barrel roll. Things apparently are good.

"Does Shoo like to play checkers?" Bigfoot Ebay asks.

"Sometimes. But mostly he likes to fly in the window and crash land on the board."

"Maybe he just needs something to pique his interest."

"I did have Chris get Ruthie to bake Shoo a set of blueberry checkers for Christmas last year, but he ate all twenty-four pieces before we could get them onto the board."

Chapter 43

First Things First

Blue Moon Inn, Monday

Chris ties his canoe up at the inn's cove dock. He exits, lifts out Gabriel's gift to Amanda, and carries it up the single-track trail through the leaf-barren aspen stand, the family of ancient forest onlookers, savants who keep watch and don't forget.

It has begun to snow lightly, the first of the year. Coming out of the tall white-barked, winter-ready trees, Chris approaches the inn and stops at the old sign post out front. He waves at Amanda, who is sitting on the top step of the inn's front porch. She waves back. He checks the eyebolts on the post where the old sign used to hang. Still good. The hooks on the new sign line up exactly. Of course. Gabriel's work, he had made both signs and the post. Chris looks again at the porch and Amanda. She is wearing her mother's old high-collared sweater.

Chris slips the hooks into place through the down-facing

bolts as the snow falls. Easy. Quiet. "*Whatever you believe is right for you*" is what Gabriel had said. After a moment more, he rolls the collar of his grandfather's colorful jacket up over his neck and looks approvingly at the newly hung sign. Good job, Gabriel. As always. He dusts the fat snowflakes from his hands and starts for the porch, leaving brown footprints on the whitening lawn as he walks.

Chris calls to Amanda, "How do you like your new sign?"

"I love it," Amanda says, "but I'm going to miss your grandfather."

"Me too."

Chris climbs the porch steps slowly, brushing the snow from his shoulders. He feels the nub of the woolen sweater and remembers Gabriel. He clears his full throat. "He said to tell you he loved you."

"And I loved him."

As he reaches the top step, Chris looks back at the special Gabriel-carved birthday front door with the closed-eyed, leafless Aspens. He smiles back a tear and sits beside Amanda.

"Did he tell you about the honeymoon?"

"He did." She leans back and laughs.

Chris leans beside her and laughs with her. He is starting to feel better. Warmer. Good.

Face-to-face now, as they had been on the street on Friday.

"Can't just anybody do a good skunk," he says and puts his hand flat on the cold porch as he had done so many years ago. "Getting that smell just right is what takes practice."

"That's what Gabriel said."

"What else did he say?"

"That both partners in a federation marriage must remain in the federation for the marriage to stay recorded down at the hall."

"Which means if Lulu or I decide to make a change, the marriage is off," Chris confirms.

"That's what he said."

He edges his hand closer to Amanda's. Amanda rubs her hands together and tucks them under her legs to warm them.

"And I have," Chris says.

"Have what?"

"Decided to make a change."

"When was that?"

"Here on this porch twenty years ago. I didn't realize it though, until just now, out there hanging that sign, looking at you in your mother's old sweater, and remembering how we were."

"What do you want to do?"

"To begin with, I'd like to move over here, to the inn. You know, with some work, you and I could make the Blue Moon into quite a showplace. In a year or so, we could add some fishing cabins along the shoreline and get Cleo to rent us some of her boats."

"You and I?"

"After we're married, I mean."

"And when would that be?"

"How about six days from now?"

"That long?"

"I'd hate to hurry things. But first thing's first." He holds out his hand to Amanda as he had twenty years ago in this very spot.

"The hand thing Gabriel told me about?"

"Yes. I promise not to pull back this time."

"And I promise not to run off." Amanda takes her warm hands from under her legs and takes Chris's cold right hand in both of her warm ones.

The light dusting of snow has turned into a blanket of

white, which now covers Good Bear Lake from the town shoreline against its Shadow Mountain backdrop to the dam on the far opposite shore, including Rainwater Island, which is no longer visible through the naked Aspen trees except for an intense tiny blue light coming from the direction of the barn. Someone inside has cracked the portal door open just enough to let out a glimmer from the reserve supply of love kept available for special occasions. Chris's guess is that someone is his beloved grandfather.

The tightly targeted beam strikes Chris and Amanda's intertwined hands. They glow faintly blue for a moment and then fade. Chris and Amanda are both now fully and permanently human, disparate parts who have become a whole.

As Chris and Amanda kiss, better by half than the rehearsal dinner kiss, the snow continues to fall. The limbs of the family of aspens that surround the inn creak their approval under the snow's weight, as the wooden aspens on the Gabriel-carved front door open their black eyes and their leaves begin to grow. Love has returned to the inn. Everything is new. Anything is possible. Just as Gabriel has predicted.

Chapter 44

It's a Girl this Time or It Goes Back

Corner Cupboard Café, several months later.

Shortly after Jack became head ranger, he took a selfie of himself as Bigfoot. He sent it to *National Geographic,* where it made the cover. That photo now hangs on the wall at the café next to Chris and Amanda's wedding picture.

Through the cook's window, Lyle reads from the weekly edition of the *Good Bear Lake News* to Ruthie, who is pregnant with baby number five.

"Get this. The US Fish and Wildlife Service has determined that the Good Bear Lake Bigfoot represents an endangered species. Subsequently, the Colorado Water Court has reversed its earlier decision and cancelled any plans the Denver Water Authority has for Good Bear Lake as an expanded water source."

Ruthie wears an apron that suggests: *It's a girl this time or it goes back.* She also reads aloud from the paper and points at a photo of Jack and Lulu in the wedding section: "After a brief honeymoon at the newly renovated Blue Moon Inn, Jack and Lulu will make their home on Rainwater Island, where Jack and Gus Cobb plan to open a regional office for PETA."

Chapter 45

Two Kinds of Hammers

All Are Welcome Church, two weeks later

Jack and Lulu's wedding is a big success. The service was a delight. Cleo sang. Becky played the piano. Dinky officiated. Shoo arrived late. Bob nearly stepped on Chip as he walked Lulu down the aisle. Tom and Becky are now engaged and planning a June wedding of their own. They go everywhere together holding hands. Humans, Francis insists, are so emotional, though he and Ebay have become somewhat of an item themselves.

Jack and Lulu's reception is being held inside the church because of the snow on the ground outside. The food table in the fellowship hall is full and includes Ruthie's blueberry muffins, Clara's banana nut bread, Cleo's fried egg sandwiches, and of course, an ample supply of store-bought Twinkies. Ruthie and Lyle are handling the food. Lyle carries little Gabriel on his chest in a baby bag. Ruthie once again looks like she may pop at any moment. Holy moly.

Chip selects a piece of banana nut bread and a chunk of blueberry muffin and, holding one in each paw, nibbles his way toward the edge of the food table. Walking off the end, he is saved by Clara, who catches him in her open purse. Sam retrieves Chip and eats the banana nut bread. He smiles at Clara as if he's enjoying it. A moment later, when Clara has moved on, he shares Ruthie's super moist muffin fragment with Chip and tucks him into his shirt pocket. Sam and Chip have agreed to agree: even though Clara's banana nut bread tends to be somewhat on the dry side, neither of them are willing to own up to that fact to a woman who carries two kinds of hammers in her purse—a ball peen and a standard claw.

Gus has traded his DWA suit coat for a blue denim jacket with PETA stitched over the pocket. He waits his turn outside the gents-only bathroom. The door opens and out comes Francis with Shoo riding on his back.

"Francis," Gus says to the dog.

Francis smiles.

No longer looking puzzled, Gus goes into the bathroom, winks at himself in the mirror, and closes the door.

Chapter 46

Nailed It

Blue Moon Inn, Jack and Lulu's wedding night

Below Gabriel's new Blue Moon Inn sign hangs a smaller wooden plaque that reads: *Chris and Amanda Rainwater, Prop.*

The last of several fishing cabins is under construction at the water's edge. Each has a hand-carved wooden sign, Chris's new hobby, over the door that identifies the cabin by its Native American name. Business should be brisk by June and continue throughout the summer and fall months, with both trout and salmon being plentiful in the lake and its river tributaries.

The largest of the new cabins, *Talaneenon,* Ute for "happy home among the rocks" has already been rented through October and into November, the month when the aspen leaves are already on the ground and the first snow is about to fall. Most of the fisher folk who come at that time of year have fished this lake before. They know that's when there's a good chance of landing a twenty-pound rainbow with their first cast.

After the reception, Jack and Lulu arrive at the inn to start their honeymoon. In an upstairs bathroom, Jack cleans his teeth.

"Don't forget to close the window," Lulu shouts from the bedroom.

"What for?" Jack replies.

"Just in case," she calls back. "We don't know where Francis and Shoo went after the reception."

"I heard they had plans with Ebay."

"Doing what?"

"Playing checkers at the hall, I would imagine."

"Did you know Francis is learning to do skunk?"

"I did. He said he was doing it in honor of Gabriel. As of last week, he still looked more like a fuzzy black Pekingese than he did a skunk. Though he's gotten the white nose stripe just about right. But he's having some trouble with the language."

"What about the smell?"

"The smell needs a lot of practice. He's squirted just about everything and everybody on the island. Bear and cougar have shown him their teeth more than once and warned him to find some other place to practice or else."

In the hallway outside the bedroom, a fuzzy black short-legged Pekingese-looking skunk with a fluffy white stripe from his tail to his nose peeks through the cracked bedroom door. Shoo and Ebay look over the skunk's shoulder.

As the bathroom light goes out, the skunk nods, as if to say, "Okay, I've got this."

Shoo echoes in a jaybird whisper. "He's got this."

The skunk shakes his black and white head and sputters, "*sssssh*."

Shoo jumps on the skunk's back, Ebay grabs his tail, and the threesome tiptoes into the bedroom.

Jack enters the bedroom, rubbing his upper arms. "Boy. It's freezing out here," he says, hurrying to bed.

Lulu is waiting for him with the covers open and welcoming. "Feels great in here," she says.

Jack jumps in. "Better, warm, and good."

"What was that?" Lulu asks.

"Something that just popped into my head when I looked at you," Jack replies and then starts sniffing. "What is that smell?" he says.

"Oh no, not again!" Lulu shouts.

Jack looks under the bed, as three sets of white eyes blink to black.

And "Nailed it," is heard spoken in broken skunk with a heavy canine accent.

The end

CPSIA information can be obtained
at www.ICGtesting.com
Printed in the USA
BVHW071156120919
558269BV00001B/144/P

9 781480 880016